The Great Fetish

The Great Fetish

L. SPRAGUE DE CAMP

DOUBLEDAY & COMPANY, INC.
GARDEN CITY, NEW YORK 1978

With the exception of actual historical persons, all of the characters in this book are fictitious and any resemblance to actual persons, living or dead, is purely coincidental.

Library of Congress Cataloging in Publication Data

De Camp, Lyon Sprague, 1907–
   The great fetish.
   I. Title.
PZ3.D3555Gr [PS3507.E2344]   813'.5'2
          ISBN: 0-385-13139-9
Library of Congress Catalog Card Number 78-1239

Copyright © 1978 by L. Sprague de Camp
All Rights Reserved
Printed in the United States of America
First Edition

The
Great Fetish

I

The clerk of the court called: "Hear, hear! On this the fifteenth day of Franklin, in the Year of Descent 1008, the District Court of the District of Skudra, in the Kralate of Vizantia, is now in session. All persons having business with this honorable court draw nigh."

As Judge Kopitar entered, the clerk added: "All rise and uncover."

The Great Fetish

Off came the sheepskin kalpaks, which most of the audience had kept on against the early-morning chill. The small peat fire in the bronze stove did little to lift this chill. Muphrid (Eta Boötis) had not yet risen. Skudra, although but a few degrees from the equator of Kforri, was cool because of its altitude. The doffing of hats revealed rows of broad skulls shaven, except for the single braided tuft, against the invasion of scalp mites. Jaws moved rhythmically, chewing quids of tobacco.

The judge said: "Clerk, lead the court in prayer."

The clerk rose and intoned: "Hail to the gods! May they preserve and watch over us; may they forgive our shortcomings. Hail to the holy trinity of Yez, Moham, and Bud! May Yustinn, god of law, guide us to just decisions. May Napoin, god of war, give us courage to face our duty. May Kliopat, goddess of love, inspire us with due sympathy towards our erring fellows. May Niuto, god of wisdom, increase our understanding. And may Froit, maker of souls, strengthen our characters to choose the right. O gods, inform us with the wisdom of the Ancient Ones, whom at the time of the Descent you did send from your paradise of Earth to teach us the arts of civilization. And look with favor upon the proceedings of this court. Amen."

The clerk looked up and said: "You may sit. . . . You there! Put out that pipe! And no spitting on the floor, either! The dignity of the court must be preserved."

The judge said: "Good morning, fellow subjects. Clerk, call the first case."

The clerk said: "The first case is that of the Kralate against Marko Prokopiu of Skudra, twenty-one years old.

The Great Fetish

It is charged that the said Marko Prokopiu did willfully and wrongfully, while employed as a teacher of boys in the public school of Skudra, teach the false and heretical doctrine called Descensionism or Anti-Evolution, namely: that the Earth, instead of being a plane of spiritual existence, from which our souls come and to which they return, is a material place or world like Kforri, and that all men, instead of having evolved under the guidance of the gods from the lower animals of Kforri, came from Earth at the time of the Descent in a flying machine. It is, moreover, charged that the said Marko Prokopiu did not only advance this false doctrine, but did also deny, contemn, and ridicule the true belief, certified by the Holy Syncretic Church of Vizantia and adopted as official by the Kral's ministers, to wit: the doctrine of Evolution. How do you plead, Marko Prokopiu?"

Marko Prokopiu, the foster son of the late Milan Prokopiu the smith, stood up. Since the year on Kforri is half again as long as that on Earth, by Terran time Marko would have been thirty-two. He was a little taller than the average but seemed short because of his abnormal breadth and girth. These were conspicuous even among Kforrians, with whom a stocky build with thick legs was general. The gravity of the planet, a third more than that of Mother Earth, had in the fifty-odd generations since the Descent eliminated spindle legs and weak hearts.

So Marko looked more like a blacksmith, which his foster father had been, than a small-town schoolteacher, despite the fact that he was no passionate exerciser. His features were rather thick, coarse, and brutal-looking. The blondness of his scalp lock distinguished him from the dark native-born Vizantians.

Although the elder Prokopius never said where they had obtained Marko, it was supposed in Skudra that he was of Anglonian or Eropian origin. These exotic antecedents had caused the intensely parochial Skudrans to look upon Marko with scorn and suspicion, even after he had grown too big and burly to be openly bullied. This treatment had caused his naturally introverted personality to become even more withdrawn.

Marko looked out over the courtroom. At the back stood the bailiff, Ivan Haliu, leaning on his billhook and wearing the same old helmet, blackened with oxidation, that Milan Prokopiu had hammered out for him years before. Ivan Haliu was looking intently towards the place where Bori Bender sat near Pavlo Arkas. The Benders and the Arkases had a feud on, and one of the two men might try to stab the other.

Marko Prokopiu picked out his friends and his foes with his glance. In the front row were his friends: his mother, small and sharp-nosed; his wife, Petronela, big and handsome; and his boarder, Chet Mongamri, the very tall man with the pointed graying Anglonian mustache. It was Mongamri who had persuaded Marko of the truth of Descensionism.

Nearly all the rest were neutral or hostile. There was Vasilio Yovanovi, the father of the pupil whom Marko had thrashed for chasing a fellow pupil with a knife. Although this beating was perfectly legal, as homicide was forbidden to minors, Vasilio Yovanovi had brought the action against Marko. The boy sat beside his father and visibly gloated. No doubt Miltiadu would call him as a witness.

And there in the bush beard and tiara of black wool was Theofrasto Vlora, Metropolitan of the Holy Syncretic Church, who had come up from Stambu to oversee the trial and harken on the prosecution. Even if the five jurors had not included Sokrati Yovanovi, a cousin of Vasilio Yovanovi, there was little chance that they would acquit him under the stern eye of the Metropolitan.

"Not guilty!" said Marko loudly, and sat down.

The judge said: "The prisoner has pleaded not guilty. Prosecutor, state your case."

Jorgi Miltiadu stood up and began: "Your honor, we expect to prove that the prisoner, contrary to the laws of the Kralate and the regulations of the school board, did willfully and wrongfully . . ." Here followed a restatement of the charge, going in more detail into Marko's iniquities. When Miltiadu had finished, the judge said to Marko's lawyer:

"Counselor, state your case."

Rigas Lazarevi rose and began: "Your honor, the defense will stipulate that my client did, in fact, teach the doctrines which he is accused—"

"Are you changing your plea to guilty?" cried Jorgi Miltiadu, leaping up like a startled tersor.

"Order," said Judge Kopitar. "Resume your seat, Master Prosecutor; you shall have your chance."

"No," said Rigas Lazarevi. "We adhere to our plea of innocence. It is on another ground altogether that we shall make our defense, namely, that the doctrines in question are true, and that not even the government has the right to compel my client to teach an untruth. For there is a higher law than princes, as our distinguished visitor the Metropolitan"—he nodded towards Theofrasto Vlora, who stared back coldly over his bristling black beard—"would be the first to assert. We shall produce—"

"I object!" cried Jorgi Miltiadu. "My honored colleague's proceeding is irregular, his arguments are irrelevant, and his implications are subversive. This is neither a churchly synod nor a meeting of the faculty of the University of Thiné to decide what is true. For our purposes, truth has been clearly set forth in section forty-two of Decree Number 230, Year of Descent 978, relating to the establishment and maintenance of a public-school system . . ."

On they went all through the long morning, back and forth, objecting, arguing, and splitting hairs. As the temperature rose, the audience squirmed on their benches and unbuttoned their shaggy sheepskin jackets. One even started to pull off his boots until Ivan Haliu stopped him by tapping his shaven skull with the butt of his billhook.

Although the audience was supposed to stay quiet, it was constantly disturbed by individual spectators pushing out of the pews for a trip to the nearest spittoon or to step outside for a nip of slivic. Others whispered and muttered until Judge Kopitar threatened to clear the courtroom.

The prosecution witnesses assembled by Jorgi Miltiadu, such as the Yovanovi boy, were not called, since the defense admitted the acts to which they were to testify. On the other hand, Miltiadu caused the question of the truth of the Descensionist doctrine to be ruled out as irrelevant, so Rigas Lazarevi never had a chance to show the books he had assembled as exhibits. Privately, Marko was just as glad. Many of these books were of foreign origin, and Marko well knew the Skudrans' suspicion of intellectual argument and hatred of anything foreign.

By dinnertime, when Muphrid stood almost overhead, all that remained were the summing-up speeches. The court recessed. Marko ate his dinner with the other prisoners: mostly cottage cheese and native Kforrian fungi, with a little mutton. Prisoner, judge, jury, witnesses, attendants, and spectators scattered to eat their dinners likewise and to stretch out for their three-hour siestas.

After siesta, Marko and the rest returned for the final arguments. Jorgi Miltiadu tore into Marko's foreignness: ". . . so this—this unspeakable *alien* not only tried to poison the minds of our youth by false and unholy beliefs. He even went to another outsider, this foreigner"—he pointed at Mongamri, who glared back—"from whom he got the damnable doctrine that all men are, in effect, aliens in their own world. Have you ever heard of anything so un-Vizantian?

"Do not be deceived by the specious arguments of my colleague, that it is the teacher's duty to follow the truth wherever it leads. Is Marko Prokopiu a god, that he can tell truth when he sees it, when wiser heads than his have been in disagreement? Obviously not. Shall we allow men tainted by alien blood to teach our children that black is white, or that Kforri is flat, or that Muphrid is cold, merely because some quirk of their natures or some insidious foreign influence has led them astray? As well hire the Einstein-worshiping witches of Mnaenn to teach their deadly arts and spells in our schools! Or the black hermits of Afka to teach that they are the chosen people of their god!

"Who shall, then, decide the truth? Why, the government of his serene majesty, Kral Maccimo, which can call upon the keenest minds in the Kralate and upon the divine wisdom of the Holy Three as incarnated in the Syncretic Church..."

On he went, Marko's heart sank. Rigas Lazarevi, when his turn came, stoutly accused Jorgi Miltiadu of prejudicing the jurors by dragging in the irrelevency of Marko's birth. But, argue as he might, he could not get around the fact that Marko had broken the law.

When the jury was sent out, the clerk announced: "The next case is that of the Kralate against Mihai Skriabi of Skudra, thirty-four years old. It is charged that the said Mihai Skriabi did, on the eleventh of Ashoka of the present year, ride his paxor down Cankar Street in Skudra while drunk; that he did moreover cause the said paxor to knock down two porch pillars from the house of Konstan Cenopulu the jeweler, causing grievous harm to the house of the said Konstan Cenopulu..."

By the time this case was over, the jurors considering Marko's case came back with their verdict:

"Guilty."

The spectators applauded. Marko cringed inwardly. What in the name of Yustinn had he ever done to them? When he got out, he would go far from this bigoted backwoods hamlet with its insensate feuds and its bitter xenophobia. He had been a fool to stay with them as long as he had, under the delusion that it was his duty to enlighten their savage brats.

The judge said: "Marko Prokopiu, I sentence you to imprisonment in the district jail for three years, beginning today, and to pay a fine of one thousand dlars, in default of which you shall spend an extra year in prison."

At this there was another spattering of applause. There were also a few murmurs of surprise at the severity of the sentence. Marko hoped that some of the spectators at least thought he was being unfairly used.

Marko caught a glimpse of Jorgi Miltiadu shaking hands with the Metropolitan, and then his own friends came up. His wife and his mother wrung his hands. Chet Mongamri said in his Anglonian accent:

"It's a damnable shame, Marko, but it will be the making of my book. Wait till you read the chapter about your trial!"

Marko gave Mongamri a sharp look. This seemed like an odd attitude, especially as Mongamri had, in a way, put Marko up to teaching Anti-Evolution.

Back in the month of Aristotle (or Ristoli as the Vizantians called it) Mongamri had arrived in Skudra with a mass of notes. He explained that he was an Anglonian who made his living by traveling about the continent and then writing and lecturing on his experiences. He was looking for a place to do a few months' quiet writing before returning to his home in Lann. As no other family in Skudra would admit a foreigner unless paid a fantastically high rent, Mongamri had naturally ended up in the house of the more tolerant and cosmopolitan Marko Prokopiu.

Many a night, Marko had sat up late with his boarder,

discussing the world beyond the Skudran Hills and the ideas that stirred men's minds in other lands. Marko had come to consider Chet Mongamri his closest friend. This was not saying much, as he had few friends of any kind and no real intimates. Now, evidently, Marko saw that to Mongamri he was at best a chapter in a book.

"Come along, Marko," said Ivan Haliu, grasping Marko's elbow.

Marko let himself be led away.

II

Marko Prokopiu sat on a stool in one corner of his cell. He rested his elbows on his knees and his chin on his fists, staring down at the floor in front of him. Outside, the rain slanted grayly past the barred window.

Although to some, solitude is a punishment, Marko was glad that he had no roommate. He wanted nothing but to sit on his stool and wallow in solitary despondency.

Behind his somberly immobile face, his mind was a stew of emotions. One of his minds was proud of him for being a martyr to truth. Another was ashamed of himself for exposing himself to punishment for the sake of a mere theory, which might not even be true. A third told him that all was over, that he might as well kill himself, while a fourth tried to console him with the thought that at least his mother and his wife, Petronela, and his friend Mongamri would remain true to him. . . .

The lock went *clank* and the door groaned open. Ristoli Vasu, the jailer, said: "Your mother is here to see you, Marko. Come."

Marko silently followed the jailer into the anteroom. There stood little Olga Prokopiu, in her old raincoat of wool impregnated with stupa gum.

"Mother!" he said. He checked an impulse to hug Olga Prokopiu when he saw that she held a cake in her hands.

"Here, Marko," she said. "Don't try to eat it all in one bite." She gave it to him with a sharp look. "Now sit down. I don't want you to fall down when you hear the news."

"What news?" said Marko, alarm stirring in his mind.

"Petronela has run off with that man Mongamri."

Marko's jaw dropped. "What . . . when . . ."

"Just an hour or two ago. That's why I came over. I told you no good would come of taking that alien into our house. Either of them. Those Anglonians have no more morals than rabbits."

Marko sat back, waiting for his stunned wits to revive. His mother said sharply:

"Now, don't sniffle. You're a grown man, and it's unseemly to show such emotion. You know what you must do."

Marko glanced around the walls of thick stupa-wood planks. "How?"

"Something will turn up." She glanced at the cake, which Marko's huge hands had badly squashed out of shape.

"Oh," said Marko. He wiped away a fugitive tear and pulled himself together. When not crushed by adversity, he could think as well as the next man. "Tell me what happened."

"After dinner I took my siesta. When I awoke, I called to Petronela to help me with the dishes, and there was no answer, nor yet when I knocked on her door. When I went into your room, there were signs of her having suddenly packed, and on the bureau I found this."

She handed her son a piece of paper, on which Petronela had written, in bad Vizantian:

My dear Marko:
Forgive my leaving you, but I cannot abide such a long wait. I am not well suited to life in Skudra anyway, and you will be happier in the long run with a woman of your own kind.

Farewell, Petronela

Marko read the note through twice, crumpled it, and threw it into a corner of the anteroom with such violence that it bounced halfway back. He said:

"Chet had left too?"

"Yes. I remembered that Komnenu's stage-wagons leave around siesta time. I hurried down Zlatkovi Street to Komnenu's stable and found him just hitching up the paxor to leave for Chef.

"There was no sign of Petronela and Mongamri, so I asked Komnenu if he had seen them. He said yes, they had just gone out on the wagon for Thiné, an hour earlier. They seemed very cheerful, laughing and holding hands. Komnenu said he supposed they were going down to Thiné to hire some lawyer more skillful than Rigas Lazarevi."

Marko picked up the crumpled sheet of note paper, smoothed it out, and read it again, as if by reading it often enough he could persuade it to change its wording. The note remained the same, and so did the searing spiritual pain that flooded his mind. Finally he said:

"What should I do, Mother?"

"Wait till tonight." She lowered her voice, glancing towards the open door into the jailer's office. "Then eat that cake, and do what seems best to you."

"Thanks. Come again soon."

"I shall see you again sooner than you think. Good-bye, and keep your character up. Your father was a man of much less intelligence than you, but he had character."

Olga Prokopiu gathered her raincoat about her and clumped out, looking too small for the voluminous garment and the heavy peasant boots, but spry for her years.

Marko returned to his cell with the note and the mangled cake. He set the cake down in a corner and himself in the opposite corner. He stared at the cake, biting his lips. He beat his fist against his palm, jumped up to pace the cell, then sat down again. He dug his knuckles into his scalp and pounded his knees with his fists. His lips writhed; his huge hairy hands clenched and unclenched.

At last, unable to control himself any longer, he jumped up with a hoarse animal yell, between a scream and a bellow. He glared at the cake, half tempted to kick or trample it—anything to work off the volcanic energies rising within him. But he retained sense enough to know he might want it later, and anyway it was his mother's gift. Instead, he caught up the stool and slammed it against the cage bars with such force that he broke off the leg by which he held it.

"Here! Here!" cried Ristoli Vasu, coming at a run. "What are you doing, Marko? Stop at once!"

Marko picked up the remains of the stool and continued to batter at the bars until the article was reduced to splinters. Then he leaped up and down on the splinters, stamping them with his boots.

"You shall have no supper!" yelled the jailer.

Marko only screamed at Vasu, rattled the cage door, kicked the walls, and pounded his own head and body with his fists.

"This is undignified!" cried Ristoli Vasu. "Marko, you're acting like a child in a tantrum!"

As these words penetrated Marko's red-hazed mind, the fit left him and he threw himself down on his pallet weeping. That, too, was un-Vizantian, but he did not care.

This, too, passed. Marko sat on the floor, having no more stool. He stared blankly, his mind filled with fantasies of horrible things he would do to Chet Mongamri and to Petronela too; only the things he would do to Petronela were not quite so horrible. He still loved her in a way.

He could not understand how such a thing had happened. Being Marko, he had simply not seen the signs of Petronela's increasing dissatisfaction with her life in Skudra, or the mutual interest that flared up between her and Mongamri as soon as the traveler moved in. It would have been hard enough for an alien girl like Petronela to get herself accepted by the Skudrans if she had married the most popular man in town. Having married one of the least popular, she found it quite impossible. To her, social acceptance and activity were of great importance.

Deprived of his supper as punishment for destroying the stool, Marko ate the cake. Nobody, he thought, could make cheese cakes as his mother could. About the third bite, as he half expected, he encountered a file. He looked at the file and then at the window bars, beyond which the rain still fell. A slow smile formed on his broad face.

∞∞∞

After midnight, Marko Prokopiu knocked on the window of his mother's bedroom. The old lady got up at once and let him in.

"Good," she said. "I knew my son wouldn't falter when his honor had to be avenged. How will you get to Thiné?"

Marko grinned. "I stole Judge Kopitar's horse and then broke into the schoolhouse and stole the school funds. I had a key to the strongbox hidden away."

"Why, Marko! What a desperate character my mild-as-milktoast son has become!"

"Huh! What have laws and morals done for me? Here,

take these. You will need something to live on. But don't spend it lavishly, or people will suspect it's not yours."

He pressed some of the stolen money upon her and stepped into the living room, plainly but decently furnished in the rustic style of the Skudran Hills. Olga Prokopiu's little tame tersor sat asleep on its perch, wrapped in its membranous wings. Marko stepped over to the big ornate chest, which Milan Prokopiu had brought all the way from Chef, to take out his father's war ax. He slid the ax head out of its leather case to see that all was well, then put it back in.

Milan Prokopiu had made this piece at the height of his powers. It had a two-foot steel shaft protruding from the wooden handle. From the other or butt end hung a leather thong to be looped over the wrist, so that if the handle slipped out of the user's grip, the weapon should not be lost.

Marko loosened the belt of his sheepskin jacket, thrust the pointed end through the loop on the back side of the case, and buckled the belt back on. The case was large enough to keep the steel spike on the end of the shaft, or the other, curved spike opposite the blade, from poking the wearer. All the steel of the ax was blued and heavily greased. So was all ironware on Kforri, where the damp, oxygen-rich atmosphere would otherwise soon rust it away to nothing.

He also took down from the wall a round steel buckler with a single handle behind its boss, a hook on the boss to hang a lantern from, and a strap to hang the shield over his back. Although no swashbuckler, he knew that the world was a rough place.

"How about some food?" he said.

"I'll get it for you," said his mother. Actually, one could make the journey from Skudra to Thiné without taking any food along, because the ubiquitous fungi provided nourishment. But it was known that a diet of fungi, unmixed with cultivated food, would in the long run cause bodily weakness and disease.

While Olga Prokopiu bustled about, Marko asked: "Was there anything to show where they were going after Thiné?"

"No. I suppose they mean to return to Anglonia."

Marko mused: "If they had gone to Chef, they would have taken ship across the Medranian Sea. As they have set out for Thiné, they would cross the Saar by caravan."

"You should know, son; you have traveled."

"I shall catch them," he said.

"See that you do." She gazed fondly at her son. "Put them to a terrible death; something I can be proud of."

Marko gathered up such spare clothing and other gear as he thought he would need, gave his mother a hug, and went out into the rain. Judge Kopitar's horse was tethered behind the Prokopiu house. Like all horses on Kforri, it was an animal of medium height and stocky, massive build.

Marko strapped his traveling bag behind the saddle, unhitched, and mounted. The horse shifted its feet and shook its head uneasily. It sensed that Marko was not its owner, but his weight discouraged it from trying to buck him off. Marko pulled the hood of his raincoat down low over his kalpak, so that it nearly hid his face, and turned the horse's head towards the road to Thiné.

Marko knew all the local roads well and had once been to Thiné, during his sabbatical two years before. He had, in fact, traveled all over Vizantia. He had been to the seaports of Chef and Stambu and Moska and Bukres, to the great stupa forests of the Borsja Peninsula, and finally to Thiné, where he had studied at the university.

At Chef, he had become acquainted with Woshon Seum, the representative of the Anglonian trading firm of Choerch and Jaex. Knowing Woshon Seum, he was bound to meet Seum's daughter Petronela. They fell in love and got married, and Marko brought her back to Skudra, to the ill-concealed consternation of his mother and his associates. He had never been popular, and marrying an alien seemed to many townsfolk like the last straw.

As he trotted through the outskirts of Skudra, Marko looked back towards the center of the town. All was dark and quiet under the pattering rain. He turned and faced the road north. Little maintenance was done on this road, so that the only check on the swift growth of the fungi was the hoofs and wheels of traffic. These merely mashed the undiscourageable vegetation into slimy pulp. Despite the calks on its shoes, the judge's horse slipped and skidded on slight slopes. On steeper ones, Marko had to get off and lead it, wishing he had been able to steal a paxor instead. This was an elephantine plant-eating reptile, which the people of Kforri domesticated and used as a heavy draft animal.

The rain let up. Marko plodded on. Wet fronds or stalks of the plants that overhung the road, like grasses and mosses enlarged to tree size, brushed against him. An active volcano glowed dull red against the underside of the rain clouds and its own smoke plume. Rifts appeared in the clouds, through which Marko glimpsed Gallio, the nearest and brightest of the three little moons, sweeping through the stars.

◈◈◈ III ◈◈◈

Ten days after leaving Skudra, on the first of Napoin or Napoleon, Marko Prokopiu jogged into Thiné. He had undergone experiences along the way, such as being pursued in the Zetskan Hills by a transor, the largest of the planet's dinosaurian predators. Several nights he had to sleep out, but he was used to roughing it. His father, a mighty hunter, had taken Marko on many camping trips.

Near Skiatho, a trio of rash robbers waylaid him and sent an arrow through his raincoat. He turned the judge's horse while tugging out his ax, and presently the archer was lying among the fungi with a cleft skull, while his fellows fled. Marko appropriated a good steel bow, a lizard-skin bow case, and a quiverful of arrows.

All this, however exciting, had no real bearing on the object of his search. When he arrived in Thiné, a spacious city built entirely of marble (a material as common on Kforri as good wood was scarce), he found himself quarters. Then he spent a day searching the city for Mongamri and Petronela.

He inquired at all the inns and promenaded the parks and shops without success. He loitered in the central square, where the caravans made up to cross the Saar to Niok and the cities of Arabistan. He asked the caravan dispatcher whether any persons like Petronela and Mongamri had gone out on the last caravan.

The man assured him that he had seen nobody like that. Moreover, the last caravan, which had left two days before, had been en route to Asham in Arabistan, far from Niok. No caravan had left for Niok in ten days, although one was due to leave in four.

Marko was sure that his quarry must still be in Thiné. They would be bound for Anglonia. Believing him still to be in jail in Skudra, they would be in no great hurry. If he did not come upon them in the next three days, he could surely intercept them when the caravan for Niok mustered in the square. He preferred to catch them sooner if possible, before the news of his escape from the jail at

Skudra should reach Thiné and a warrant be issued for his arrest.

He was also anxious not to let them escape from Vizantia, for he had heard that in some other countries homicide was a criminal as well as a civil offense. And while Marko had, right after his escape from jail, been in a mood to defy all rules because of the injustice he felt, his basically law-abiding nature had now had time to reassert itself.

On his third day in Thiné, after a perfunctory stroll about the central part of the town to look for his wife and her paramour, he rode out to the university grounds. There he hunted up the professor who had been his faculty adviser when he had studied here.

In his office, Gathokli Noli was entertaining a stranger, a small, gray-haired man with a bulging dome of a cranium, a sharp nose, and a receding chin. The man wore Anglonian clothes: knitted trunk-hose and shoes with flaring tops and pointed toes, instead of the baggy checkered pants tucked into the tops of heavy boots, usual in Vizantia. The stranger wore eyeglasses, a Mingkwoan invention still rare in Vizantia. He spoke with an Anglonian accent, reducing the rolled Vizantian *r* to a soft, vowel-like sound. Instead of his wearing the Vizantian scalp lock, his hair was cut to a uniform length of a half inch, so that it stood up in a stiff gray brush.

"By the Great Fetish of Mnaenn, it's Marko!" said Gathokli Noli. "Come in, old man. Marko, this is Dr. Boert Halran of Lann, the eminent philosopher."

Marko acknowledged the introduction with the natural

dignity of the Vizantian hillman. "What brings you to Thiné, Dr. Halran?"

"I have come to purchase stupa gum, sir."

"Isn't it for sale in Anglonia?" asked Marko.

"Yes, but only in minute quantities. I require a considerable amount, so it is cheaper for me to come all this distance to obtain it at a wholesale price."

"Are you using it for some experiment?"

"Yes, sir; the most portentous experiment of the era, if I may so assert." Halran shimmered with self-satisfaction.

"Indeed, sir? May I ask what it is?"

"Have you ever heard of a balloon?" asked Halran.

"No. The word is unfamiliar to me."

"Well, are you familiar with the hypothesis that, if one could inclose hot air in a bag, the bag would rise like a bubble in water?"

"There was some talk about it at the university when I was here. As I was immersed in courses in pedagogy, I didn't go very far into science."

"Well, I have actually accomplished it."

"Made a bag rise?"

"Yes, bags of various magnitudes." The little man glowed with enthusiasm. "One of the largest raised me to an altitude of a hundred feet and stayed up for two hours. It frightened the peasants to death when it came down in their fields, so my next model I tethered by its drag rope to keep it from being wafted anywhither.

"My next step will be to construct a balloon large enough to raise the weight of several individuals. The bag has already been sewn together; there remains but the matter of the stupa gum to render it airtight."

"How do you heat this air?" asked Marko.

"By means of a large peat stove."

"I see. But after the machine has risen, won't the air inside cool off and let you down again?"

"Eventually, yes. But this balloon is equipped with a smaller stove suspended above the car, so that, by feeding more hot air into the bag, I can maintain altitude much longer."

"I should love to see it," said Marko.

"If you are in Lann about the third of Perikles, come around. On that day, I intend to inflate my balloon for a flight to the Philosophical Convention at Vien."

Marko said: "I have heard of these philosophical conventions and should love to attend one. How do you do it? I mean, what does one have to be or to do to get in?"

"Merely pay a small registration fee."

"Is that all? No special degree is required?"

"No; we philosophers are only too glad to have the public take an interest in our accomplishments. These conventions have been in operation only about ten years, but they grow bigger every year. This year there are rumors that a pair of philosophical brothers from Mingkwo will bring some sensational inventions they have developed. If, that is, the Prem of Eropia does not choose that time to start a war or massacre his enemies."

"Is he a dangerous man?" said Marko, who had heard only vaguely of the vagaries of Alzander Mirabo.

Halran whistled, rolled up his eyes, and held his palms together as in prayer. "Extremely dangerous. Shrewd, ruthless, unpredictable, and insatiably ambitious. If he thinks you stand in his way, he may entertain you one day and charm you with his affability, and the next have your head hacked off in the main square of Vien.

"The Chamber elected him Prem because he promised to break the power of the magnates, which he did. Then he got all their lands and manufactories into his own hands. Since then, he has ruled the country with an even more iron hand than the magnates did."

"Why don't the Eropians revolt?" asked Marko.

"Them? Oh, most of them like him. He poses as the champion of the masses against their exploiters and so has achieved a meretricious popularity—"

"He has effected some real reforms, too," interjected Noli.

Halran shrugged. "If you consider those worth his turning the judicial system into an instrument for punishing his personal opponents. But his ambitions do not stop there. He has been strengthening his army lately, and rumors hint at an invasion of Iveriana. Of course, when my balloon is perfected, it will make war impossible. But there are still many details to be worked out."

"How will it make war impossible, sir?" said Marko.

"By making it too risky and too horrible for men to endure. How could any government defend its land against a horde of enemies rising in balloons on the windward side of the border and descending anywhere in the realm? This invention will compel the nations to unite to abolish war."

Marko inquired: "Have you got your stupa gum yet, sir?"

"No; it will take some days. The Kral's government requires much signing of papers before it will let me export the material, which is curious when you consider that stupa-tree products are the main export of Vizantia."

"Not so odd," said Gathokli Noli. "These forms are to make sure nobody fells a stupa tree on his own, contrary to law." He turned to Marko. "And now let me ask: What brings you down from your misty mountains? How is your handsome wife?"

From a stranger, Marko would have resented a question about his wife. Vizantians considered it indelicate to talk about marital relationships. After all, everybody knew what married people did. But Noli was an old friend, and the people of the university were a bit looser in such matters than Marko's fellow Skudrans.

As for Halran, it was notorious that Anglonians had no such inhibitions. Marko gulped and replied:

"As a matter of fact, it is she that brings me here. She decided she liked one of her fellow countrymen better than me, and I'm following them to send them to Earth." He touched his ax.

Halran started visibly. Noli merely raised an eyebrow. "Oh? I shouldn't have mentioned the matter, had I guessed this complication. I'm sorry for your trouble and wish you success."

"Have you seen either of them?" Marko, twirling an imaginary mustache, described his faithless friend Mongamri.

"No-o," said Gathokli Noli. "But I'll keep a watch for him."

Halran said: "By Kliopat, you two talk calmly enough about slaying a man. Do you really mean that, or is this a jest?"

"No joke at all, sir," said Marko. "What I plan to do is not only legal; it's practically compulsory. If I didn't make every effort to kill the guilty pair, I should be held in aversion and contempt."

Halran shuddered. "In Anglonia we consider such a thing barbarous."

"No doubt, sir. Of course, an ignorant hillbilly like myself has no right to speak. But, while in Anglonia you place an absurdly high value on human life, you don't take honor and purity so seriously as we do."

"But my dear fellow, there is no comparison between killing a fellow being and giving one of the other sex a few minutes' harmless pleasure."

"Harmless pleasure! That only proves how depraved and immoral . . ." began Marko with heat, but Gathokli Noli interrupted:

"Other lands, other customs. I'll tell you: Why don't you, Marko, promise to spare the man who cuckolded you while Boert swears eternal chastity?"

"But I am a married man!" protested Halran.

Marko said: "That would not be fair. At Dr. Halran's age—"

"I like that!" cried Halran. "What do you know about my private life, Master Prokopiu?"

"Gentlemen, gentlemen," said Noli. "Let's change the subject, which is becoming just too indelicate. Are you attending commencement tomorrow, Marko?"

"I hadn't known you were having it," said Marko, "but I shall be glad to come." Privately he thought this a good chance to run into Mongamri and Petronela.

"As a diploma holder," said Noli, "you will be deemed

a member of the university, ranking with the two-year sub-bachelors. You shall therefore sit with the graduates and wear an academic robe."

"Oh," said Marko. "Had I known, I should have brought mine from Skudra, but as it is . . ."

"That's all right; I'll get you one," said Noli. "Meet me here at the third hour tomorrow."

※※※

Marko spent the rest of the day in a further futile search for his victims. The next morning, he appeared at Gathokli Noli's office at the appointed time.

Gathokli Noli hung upon him the short black cape of the holder of a mere diploma in education, and himself donned the sweeping scarlet cassock of a full professor. Boert Halran appeared too, in the purple surplice of an Anglonian Doctor of Philosophy.

They solemnly tipped their academic hats to each other and marched out and across the campus to the commencement grounds. Over these had been erected a great canvas canopy; for, although Muphrid showed his face at that time, it was too much to expect the heavens of Thiné to refrain from raining for half an hour at a stretch.

Gathokli Noli explained as they walked: "Sokrati Popu will deliver the commencement address and receive an honorary doctorate. That should cause some uproar."

"Why?" asked Boert Halran. "Is this Popu unpopular?"

Gathokli Noli rolled his eyes. "He's the leader of the Distributionist movement."

"What is that?" inquired Halran. "I have sufficient

difficulty keeping up with the politics of my own land, let alone that of others."

Gathokli Noli explained: "As you know, the main wealth of the Kralate lies in the great stupa forests of the Borsja Peninsula."

"Yes."

"Besides the stupa gum you are after, one of those trees contains enough wood to build a small city. Nowhere else in the world, as far as it has been explored, do real trees grow to a fraction of such size."

"I see," said Halran.

"Well," continued Noli, "a generation ago, private lumbermen were making serious inroads into the forests. The then Kral, Jorgi the Second, was a far-sighted man. He saw that the trees were being cut faster than they grew and that the whole process was wastefully managed. So he nationalized the forests and set up a program of controlled cutting and planting.

"That worked until the present Kral came to the desk. Kral Maccimo"—Noli glanced about—"is a man of, say, a character different from that of his father. There have been complaints that the forest service is loaded with political hangers-on who do nothing but shuffle papers. Therefore a group of magnates started a movement to have the government sell the forests to them cheaply.

"To promote their idea, they take advantage of the Kralate's financial troubles, the complaints of people who wish unlimited stupa wood for building, the pressure of the lumberjacks' guild, and anything else that will serve their turn. But the students are mostly Retentionists—that is, Anti-Distributionists—so there may be a disturbance."

They came to the commencement grounds, where the public seats were fast filling. Gathokli Noli showed Marko and Halran their proper places. Marko found himself in a whole section of diploma capes. As he sat down, the handle of his ax, hitherto hidden by his cape, touched the leg of the man beside him. This man stared and whispered:

"You should not have brought that thing in here!"

Marko smiled and shrugged vaguely. He began peering at the other sections from under the brim of his academic hat.

The professors were assembling on the platform. Undergraduates were pushing into the large front-center section reserved for them. They indulged in much shoving and horseplay, which the admonitions of the beadles did little to check.

Then Marko saw Chet Mongamri and Petronela come in through one of the main entrances and take places with the rest of the public. They were a long way from Marko and to his left rear, so that he had to crane his neck to see them. His breath quickened, and he turned his head to the front again lest they recognize him. A cold rage filled him, so that he hardly heard what went on around him. He clenched his fists and bit his lips. The men next to him edged away from his apocalyptic aspect.

At last everybody was in place. The beadles stood at attention at the ends of the aisles, holding their staves as if they had been pikes. The president of the university, Mathai Vlora, opened the proceedings.

The university's band played "Vizantia Victorious." The president introduced the Bishop of Thiné. The bishop invoked the blessings of the gods upon the university and its students—especially the blessings of Dui, the god of education.

The president gave an opening address, which seemed to Marko to say nothing very eloquently, and began introducing the recipients of honorary degrees. There was Maccimo Vuk, the distinguished assassin, who had given the university ten thousand dlars. There was Ivan Laskari, who claimed to have proved that atoms existed. And, after several others had been honored, there was Sokrati Popu. His only qualification seemed to be that, as head of the Distributionists, he stood to become the richest man in the nation if his scheme went through.

Sokrati Popu was a short man with a large head, bald and jowly. He let the president drape the yellow stole of the honorary doctorate around his neck. They tipped their academic hats. Sokrati Popu stepped to the lectern at the front of the platform, laid a sheaf of manuscript down in front of him, raised a lorgnette to his eyes, and began to read the commencement address.

"Young men and fellow subjects," he began in a rasping monotone, "it gives me great pleasure . . ."

After several paragraphs of the usual clichés of commencement oratory, he got down to business: ". . . Vizantia stands at the fork of the road. Which horn of the dilemma shall we take? One hurls us into the swamp of state monopoly, which has crushed the proud nation of Eropia, once a leader of civilization, to a nightmare of bureaucratic stagnation. The other leads the ship of state back along the highroads of private enterprise, which stand guard at the shrine of economic sanity—"

At that instant, a student stood up in the undergraduate section and threw a tersor's egg at Sokrati Popu. The missile missed its target and spattered against the wall of the Liberal Arts Building, which formed a background for the ceremony.

Instantly the two beadles nearest to the undergraduate section plunged into the black-cloaked mass and pounced upon the student. They dragged him out, despite the efforts of the other undergraduates to trip and impede them, and hustled him up an aisle to the exit.

"There's one who gets no degree today," said the man beside Marko who had objected to his ax.

Sokrati Popu resumed his discourse, but now the undergraduates began to mutter in cadence: "I—want—money; I—want—money; I—want—money . . ."

The beadles, hovering on the fringes of the undergraduate section, reached in and whacked a couple of the noisier of the mutterers with their staves. The chant subsided; Sokrati Popu doggedly resumed:

"What do these benighted bureaucrats really want? To save the stupa forests for posterity as they say? Nonsense! We can never exhaust the stupa forests, and anyway what has posterity ever done for us? The bureaucrats want power! Make no mistake, my ardent young friends—"

Another student threw another tersor's egg. More beadles tried to reach him, but now the undergraduates clutched them and pulled them down. Marko glimpsed a beadle's arm flailing about with its staff and then disappearing under the black, billowing mass. The students chanted:

"Wood—for—Popu; wood—for—Popu; wood—for—Popu . . ."

Others stood up and hurled not only eggs but also bits of edible fungi in various states of decay. The president popped up and shouted threats at the undergraduates, who made rude noises and threw more missiles. These spattered not only Popu but also the president, the faculty, and the other guests. The president roared orders to the beadles, who waded into the throng, swinging their staves at every undergraduate head they saw.

The fight boiled out into the aisles. Through it all, Sokrati Popu stood behind his lectern, raw tersor egg running down his face, and doggedly continued his address. Marko could see his mouth move, even though he could not hear any words.

Marko tore his attention away from the fracas in front to look back into the audience. They were all standing up to see better. Among the heads he glimpsed the sweeping Anglonian mustache of Chet Mongamri.

Knowing his duty, Marko rose with pounding heart, unsnapped the flap of his ax sheath, and pushed his way out into the aisle. He dodged a couple of fights, ran up the aisle all the way to the rear, crossed over to the left side of the audience, and started down the left interior aisle. As he ran, he drew the ax from its case.

Marko dodged around beadles dragging undergraduates out and bore down upon Chet Mongamri, who had taken an aisle seat. He was sighting on the back of Mongamri's head for a place to sink his ax blade when a beadle, taking cognizance of Marko's homicidal intentions, released his undergraduate and grabbed Marko's sleeve, shouting:

"Ho, there, you!"

Marko jerked his arm free and pushed the man in the chest, bowling him over, then turned back to resume his charge. But the beadle shouted, and others joined in. The noise down front had momentarily subsided, so that this sudden outburst caused many of those farther forwards to turn their heads rearwards. One of these who looked around was Chet Mongamri.

Marko saw Mongamri's jaw sag and his eyes bug as he recognized Marko. Marko swung the ax high and bounded forward. Beside Mongamri, Petronela shrieked.

Mongamri stepped out into the aisle and ran towards the stage ahead of Marko. A lean man, taller than Marko, he could show a remarkable turn of speed. Marko pounded after, and the beadles ran after Marko.

Mongamri leaped to the left end of the platform and started to run across it. Marko jumped up after him. In the middle of the stage, President Vlora was still shouting directions to his beadles and threats to his students, while Sokrati Popu continued to deliver his inaudible speech. On the upstage part of the platform, the faculty and the distinguished guests were crouched on their knees, holding the light chairs in front of them as shields against the rain of missiles.

Mongamri pushed between the president and Popu and ran on to the right end of the platform. The president and Popu looked around at this interruption. Both saw Marko approaching with his ax. With a scream of terror, Sokrati Popu turned and dove in amongst the cowering faculty, while Mathai Vlora leaped off the platform into the boiling, black-cloaked mass of undergraduates.

Marko ran on. He reached the right end of the platform

to see Chet Mongamri streaking back up the right interior aisle. The fellow was actually gaining on him. Marko sprang down from the edge of the platform and gathered his great muscles for a desperate sprint, when his head exploded and he knew no more.

※※※

When Marko Prokopiu regained consciousness, he was first aware of lying on a bed and then of a splitting headache. He raised a hand to his head and discovered that on the crown, just in front of the scalp lock, it bore a lump the size of a tersor egg.

"Waking up, eh?" said a voice with an accent. After a few seconds, Marko identified the voice as that of Boert Halran, the little Anglonian philosopher.

Marko groaned and sat up. "Where is this?" he asked.

"This is my room," said Halran.

"How did I get here? The last thing I remember was chasing that lecher Mongamri—"

"A beadle fractured his staff on your head as you ran past him. He would have arrested you, because it transpires that in Thiné there is some quaint law that renders it a misdemeanor to kill people during commencement exercises, church services, and other public occasions. But the riot became general, and the beadle had his hands full with whacking undergraduates. I thought only Anglonian students did that sort of thing."

"I don't know Anglonia, but the Thinean undergraduates are the rowdiest lot of savages in the Kralate. I had to knock several of them cold when I was here before. Go on, please."

"Well, Noli and I fought our way through the mob and carried you to his office; or rather, we got an undergraduate to help us, because you are the heaviest man I ever tried to lift. Then we could not bring you back to consciousness. You must have had a slight concussion."

"Where's my ax?" said Marko.

"Here is that murderous monstrosity. While you were in the office, some of your local police agents came by looking for you. Noli hid you in his closet. They explained they had a warrant for your arrest, which had been sent down from Skudra for breaking jail there. I did not realize you were such a calloused character."

"I didn't use to be," groaned Marko. "I was only trying to do my duty."

"Well, they informed us about your having been sentenced for teaching Descensionism, too, and Noli told them he had no conception of where you were. As he explained to me subsequently, he is an Evolutionist himself; but, believing in freedom of speech, he thought himself obliged to protect you. Finally, they departed to scour the town for you. Then Noli asked me to conceal you. I do not like to become involved in the domestic quarrels of another country, but I owe Noli many favors and so let myself be persuaded."

Marko's mind had begun to work, despite the fact that an invisible smith seemed to be using his head for an anvil. "What day is this?"

"The fifth of Napoleon. You have been unconscious for almost exactly twenty-four hours."

Marko groaned. "They'll have left on the caravan! I must get my horse!"

"You will not find your horse, I fear."

"What? Why not?"

"The officers informed us they had recovered a horse you had stolen from some magistrate in Skudra. Is that the one you refer to?"

"Yes." Marko held his head for a few seconds. "Do you know when the next caravan leaves for Niok?"

"On the eleventh. That is the one I shall take."

"Then I shall go too."

"Oh?" said Boert Halran with a note of alarm in his voice.

"Why not? I can pay my way, and it looks as though the Kralate would be too warm for me for a while." Marko stood up and cautiously moved his head. "A little dizzy, but it will pass. I'll go to my own quarters so as not to encumber you any more, sir."

"Are you feeling all right?" said Halran. "It would be most inexpedient for you to lose consciousness in the street."

"It will take a thicker club than that to crack my skull. Thank you for your valued hospitality."

"You are welcome, my friend. Oh, before you go, Noli asked me to collect from you the price of that academic hat he obtained for you. The blow ruined it, and if you do not pay for it he will be compelled to do so."

Marko paid and departed. He got back to his own room without encounters and spent most of the next five days there. He would have liked to search the town some more, to make sure that Mongamri and Petronela had in fact departed on the caravan of the fifth. But he feared being recognized.

IV

As Muphrid rose on the eleventh of Napoleon, Marko Prokopiu, carrying his bag, came to the central square, where the caravan was mustering. Having no mount, he would have to buy a seat on a camel to Niok.

The caravan conductor, a swart Arabistani, stood at the center of a knot of travelers, assigning them their places and collecting fares. Among the passengers, Marko recognized Boert Halran. Halran had, besides his own luggage, a large hand cart on which stood four huge jugs. A pair of workmen leaned against the wheels of the cart.

Four archers in well-oiled hauberks of chain mail squatted on their heels, holding the reins of their horses. These men were supposed to protect the caravan from robbers and wild beasts. Because of the protection they afforded, the conductor collected fares even from those who had their own mounts or vehicles for the privilege of accompanying the rest.

"All right," said the conductor to Halran. "I'll hang these four jugs on one of my camels and give you a seat on another. Can you manage a camel?"

"Yes."

"Then let me see, who shall take the other seat of old Mutasim? . . . You!" The conductor addressed Marko. "Do you wish a seat too?"

"Yes," said Marko. "To Niok."

"Can you drive a camel?"

"I've never tried."

"Then you can't. You shall take the back seat on this beast. I ought to charge you extra fare because of your weight, but I'm in a generous mood."

Halran looked quizzically at Marko. "You seem to be my fate, my sanguinary young friend. Have you ever traveled by camel?"

"No, sir."

"You have much to learn, then. Strap your bag on here."

Boert Halran showed Marko how to stow himself and his gear aboard their beast. Then he went to help the two workmen, the conductor, and the caravan dispatcher to manhandle the jars off the cart and sling them on the next camel astern. When this had been done, he came back and climbed into the front seat on Marko's camel.

The caravan dispatcher looked at the big vertical sun dial, which rose out of the ornamental fountain at the center of the square. "Only fifteen minutes late," said he to the conductor. "If I live long enough, I shall get a caravan off on time yet."

The dispatcher smote a gong near the sun dial with a long-handled mallet. The conductor shouted orders. With a chorus of snorts and moans, the camels rose. Marko, forewarned, held the handhold in front of him and so was not thrown off, although one other passenger was. The camel behind Marko's rose, laden with the four amphorae of stupa gum.

Marko's saddle was part of an elaborate structure, which fitted around the camel's forward hump, with a gap in the middle through which the shaggy apex of the hump projected. Behind the hump was one seat, on which Marko sat. Forward was another, on which sat Boert Halran with his feet resting on the back of the camel's neck.

The caravan consisted mainly of thirty-two camels, carrying riders or loads. There were also a wagon pulled by two camels, a carriage drawn by a pair of horses, two other horses with riders, and the four mounted archers. The camels had little sticks tied to their tails with flags to indicate ownership.

"Go!" cried the conductor, whose name was Slim Qadir. The procession formed as mounts and vehicles took their places in the line, which crawled out of the main square of Thiné.

They plodded out of the square, through the streets, and along the west road. They passed through the avenue of stupas that Jorgi the First had planted many years before. These were mere saplings compared to those of the Borsja Peninsula, none being over twelve feet in diameter.

As the caravan climbed towards the Pindo Hills, a northward continuation of the Skudran and Zetskan hills, the trees became smaller and sparser. Their place was taken by the crowding, bamboolike kackinsoni. The sky clouded over; the rain began. They sloshed through the Borgo Pass, between the volcanoes Elikon and Parnasso, and down the long slope towards the Saar.

On the following day after siesta, Marko saw the Saar for the first time. The sandy soil stretched away to the horizon, sparsely covered with patches of phosphor grass and little bat-veiled fungi. Here and there rose a clump of the onion-mushroom, *Scallionis*. Slim Qadir warned his party that the local variety, although it looked just like other onion-mushrooms, was deadly poisonous. When they got closer to the Medranian Sea, the onion-mushrooms would become safely edible again.

Hours ticked slowly past as they jounced across the vast waste. Its aridity was due to the long spur of hills, which the Equatorial Range thrust northward from the spine of the Borsja Peninsula. The Skudran and Zetskan and Pindo hills were links in this chain, which wrung most of the moisture out of the prevailing northeasterly winds in passing over them.

The terrain varied from hour to hour. Sometimes it was flat or gently rolling sandy country with scattered fungi and spiny shrubs. Sometimes there were lifeless dunes. They passed jagged outcrops of rock and clumps of low, steep-sided hills, and sometimes a group of smoking volcanic cones. Little life was to be seen, save an occasional herd of dromsors, slender running lizards something like a reptilian ostrich in shape, or a flock of batlike tersors flying overhead.

Once they were well into the Saar, Slim Qadir forbade cooking fires. "Robbers," he explained. "Zaki Riadhi's band lurks in these hills."

"Oh, mercy!" said Halran. "I hope we shall not encounter them."

North of the L-shaped peninsula of Vizantia lay the Khlifate of Arabistan, including not only the base of the peninsula but also the great offshore island of Mahrib. The territory of the Khlifate extended southward along the shores of the Medranian Sea to take in the whole Saar. Under the feeble and disorderly government of the Khlif, Yubali the Third, the Saar was for practical purposes not governed at all.

During the first days after leaving Thiné, Marko learned how to manage a camel. He also tried to engage Boert Halran in conversation. Although a man who did not make friends easily, he felt such a wealth of mutual interests with Halran that he had no hesitation in talking to him. In fact, Marko became positively garrulous, babbling openly about his ideas of man and the universe.

Halran, normally a much less inhibited person, remained aloof and taciturn. The philosopher's attitude became so marked that Marko, realizing, finally said:

"Dr. Halran, have I been—ah—have I been boring you? Have I offended you in some way? I know I'm just—just a backwoods bumpkin—"

"No, sir," said Halran. "I find you, yourself, a personable and likable young man. It is your bloodthirsty social ethos that I take exception to."

"Oh? Why, I wouldn't harm *you!*"

"You do not understand. You are proceeding to Anglonia, where murder is the most serious crime on the calendar, with the avowed intention of killing this fugitive pair. When you have done so, the law will take you and hang you. Because you have associated with me, it might be proved that I had knowledge of your designs. In that event, the law is likely to throw me into prison for the rest of my life as well."

"But you are not asked to take any part in this deed!"

"Nevertheless, I shall be what our law calls an accessory before the fact. By merely keeping silent and failing to turn you over to the law to imprison or deport, I incur part of your guilt. Now do you see what a difficult position you place me in? For all I know, you may decide your only security lies in killing everyone having knowledge of your intentions, and split my skull with that frightful cleaver."

Marko was shocked. "I didn't know that! I'm—I don't know what to say. I wouldn't antagonize you for anything."

"Well, you see how things look to others."

"I know. I have never understood how other people's minds work. But look, doesn't an Anglonian whose wife has been stolen have any recourse? Is he expected to say merely, 'Yes, sir, thank you, sir, is there anything else, sir?'"

Halran shrugged. "In the first place, our law does not class people as property. So, as one can only steal property, one cannot 'steal' a wife or husband. And the mere fact that one's mate prefers somebody else does not constitute damage."

"Not damage? Isn't breaking up a home and family damage?"

"Well, if she were kept against her will, your life with her would be unhappy anyway, so is it not better to let her go? If you can show actual damage—say from loss of her services as housekeeper—you can recover that amount by a suit at law. But our courts are slow and expensive, and the amount awarded is usually trivial."

"But your loss of honor—"

"Honor is a subjective, intangible loss. Therefore our laws take no cognizance of it."

"One might say," said Marko, "that most Anglonians have so little honor that it isn't worth bothering about. If you'll excuse my saying so. Isn't there some maxim about the law's not taking account of trifles?"

Halran laughed, throwing back his head. "I believe there is. However, we do think we have, by eliminating all these subjective and sentimental considerations like 'honor' and 'purity,' attained a degree of rationality in our legal system surpassed by no other nation."

"It may be rational, but how about the results? Many

people are naturally lustful and polygamous. So we set up a strict barrier of custom and law to restrain these impulses. You say, what harm does it do to indulge them, and let people do as they please?

"As a result, you Anglonians trade mates every year, and your children grow up a feckless, irresponsible lot from always changing parents and never having any consistent rules to obey. We have a saying, 'Distrust three things: a wild onion-mushroom, a quiet volcano, and an Anglonian's word.'"

"Oh, we are not so bad as that. Wait until you have visited Anglonia before you condemn us."

"I shall be most interested to see it, sir."

"For instance," said Halran, "I have been married to the same woman for fifteen years, and each of us had been married only twice before we met each other. True, our friends do regard us as a trifle quaint."

"Well, Anglonians shouldn't go marrying Vizantians and then revert to the Anglonian moral standard. We don't stand for that sort of thing. Petronela knew I expected to be her first, last, and only man—"

"What reason have you to believe you were her first? No normal Anglonian girl marries before she has accumulated some experience."

"Good gods!" groaned Marko. "I never thought of that!"

This discussion went on for several days. Finally Marko said: "Sir, I still think it my duty to kill the guilty pair. But I don't wish either to be hanged myself—I'm not really brave, I fear—or to get you into trouble. So I've given up the idea of killing them, at least unless they return to Vizantia, where it would be legal."

"Good!" said Halran. "I congratulate you on your good sense. Then you will yourself return to Vizantia as soon as we attain the other side of the Saar?"

"No, sir. You forget I have a jail sentence hanging over me there. Could a man like myself make a living in Anglonia?"

"Mmm—I suppose you could. There are various possibilities such as mercenary soldier, teacher of Vizantian, and so forth."

"Besides," said Marko, "even if I don't kill Mongamri and my wife, it is my duty to confront them and demand an explanation."

"What is there to explain, except that she prefers him to you?"

"Well—ah—perhaps Petronela, having come to know Mongamri better, would like to come back to me," said Marko wistfully.

"Do you learn nothing from one painful experience? I advise you to have nothing to do with them," said Halran. "A conflict might arise that would eventuate in somebody's being injured despite your good intentions."

"Isn't one even allowed to kill in self-defense?"

"Yes, but the burden of proof is on the slayer. Forget them."

"I can't. You have no idea how ashamed I am at giving up my resolution to kill them. I'm a weak, wavering, immoral, dishonorable knave. The least I can do is to find and confront them."

They rode on. Once he had shelved his homicidal resolution, Marko found Halran perfectly friendly. The little man was not well adjusted to the rigors of caravan travel, having a fastidious dislike of soiling his hands and hating the discomforts of camel riding and sleeping out. On the other hand, he mixed well with the other people and was always organizing them into teams and groups for any purpose that arose, from fetching water to folk singing. His favorite expression was "Let us get organized," and he could always find some way of making tasks lighter by planning them.

"Indolence," he told Marko, "is the mother of invention, and I am the laziest philosopher in Anglonia."

He was also an expert card player. In three days, before the other caravaners learned to be wary of him, he had won half his fare from them in small games.

On the sixth day, the caravan stopped for its siesta at the Oasis of Siwa. The oasis lay in a wide basin, broken by irregular outcrops. From a distance, it was distinguished from the rest of the barren scene by clumps of kackinsoni, whose spearlike leaves added a splotch of green to the otherwise drab, gray-and-buff scene.

Slim Qadir rode his camel up to the water hole and made it lie down, shouting to the others to keep the animals back until some water had been scooped up for the people. There was much noise and confusion, neighing of horses and burbling of camels struggling to get to the water and shouts of their riders and drivers trying to keep them back.

Marko heard Slim Qadir yelling to his guards in Arabistani. Marko knew only a few words, but the intent seemed to be that they should get out to the edges of the oasis to guard the party against surprise attack, instead of flopping down on their bellies to have the first swill of water.

The camel ridden by Halran and Marko, together with the led camel bearing the jugs of stupa gum, were near the tail of the procession. From the back seat, Marko said:

"Hurry, Dr. Halran, or the water will be all muddied."

"There is plenty of time," said Halran.

When Marko and Halran were almost the only persons in the caravan still mounted, somebody shouted and pointed. Marko heard the drumming of hoofs. As he turned to look, there came the snapping of many bowstrings and the harsh swish of arrows. The sound of an arrow's striking flesh caused him to look down to see one embedded in the side of his camel, just below his left foot. The camel started and roared.

A band of mounted men had ridden out from behind the nearest outcrop and now were charging the oasis. They were small dark men on stocky ponies. Besides the usual sheepskins, some wore colored scarves around their heads and other bits of incongruous finery.

The people of the caravan seemed to lose all sense. They rushed about, screaming and trying to climb back on their mounts. Halran emitted a wordless squeak and tugged wildly on Mutasim's halter.

Marko, however, remained steady. He thought what he ought to do and set about doing it. He drew from its case the steel bow he had taken from the robber near Skiatho and began shooting at the oncoming attackers.

"What shall we do?" cried Halran. "What shall we do? They will kill us! I am terrified!"

"Turn this beast around," said Marko.

Marko saw his fourth arrow strike one of the Arabistanis, who were now close. Some of them swerved around the oasis, shooting. A few rode right through it, spearing and swording as they went. People shrieked.

Marko continued shooting, squirming about in his seat to loose arrows wherever he saw a robber. Those that had charged through the oasis circled around and galloped back. In the rear of the charge rode a man on a white horse, clad from head to foot in fine chain mail, with an inlaid steel helmet on his head. Perhaps, thought Marko, Zaki Riadhi himself.

Marko reached for an arrow to try a long shot at the leader of the robbers and glanced at his quiver. This was his last arrow. As he nocked it, he had a glimpse of one of Slim Qadir's archers lying on the ground while a mounted robber jabbed at him; of another flinging himself on his horse and galloping off into the desert. The fat merchant from Begrat ran past Marko's camel until a robber's lance took him in the back and hurled him prone.

Another robber rode up alongside Marko's camel, fumbling with an arrow. As he came abreast, he got it nocked and raised the bow. Marko, who had started to sight on the leader in armor, brought his aim down and released at the near robber. The arrow hit the man in the upper chest, while the robber's own arrow hissed past Marko's head.

The robber dropped his bow, threw out his arms, and fell out of the saddle. The riderless horse trotted past, right under Marko. Marko hesitated, thinking out a plan.

Boert Halran had gotten the riding camel turned around, so that it faced away from the oasis. The burden camel plodded after. Marko hung his bow on the pommel in front of him and leaped off the back of the camel onto that of the horse, which staggered under the impact. He unslung his buckler, drew out his ax, and called up:

"Make all the speed you can. I'll try to keep off the Arabis."

Marko gathered up the reins with his shield hand and turned the horse. The robbers were scattered all over the oasis, within and without it. Some were killing the remaining caravaners.

A couple fought Slim Qadir himself, who stoutly swung a scimitar with his back to a clump of kackinsoni until another robber thrust a lance through the clump into Slim's back. Down he went.

Other robbers rode about in aimless fashion. The arrows had ceased to whiz because the archers, like Marko, had exhausted their quivers.

At the sight of Marko's camels trotting off, the armored man shouted and pointed. A little knot of horsemen gathered and cantered towards Marko and the camels, opening out into a line abreast.

Marko kicked his horse's ribs with the broad, shovel-shaped butt ends of his stirrups. The animal started so suddenly that Marko almost fell off backwards. He guided the horse straight towards the armored man, making practice swings with his ax.

The Great Fetish

Between Marko and the robber chief, the line of horsemen galloped nearer, swords waving. One, a little ahead of the others, swung a scimitar in a downright cut at Marko's head. Marko caught the blow with a clang on his buckler, at the same time striking forehand with his ax. The ax cut through the corner of the shield of paxor hide, which the robber lowered to protect his body, and went on into the man's ribs. The force of the blow, driven by Marko's massive muscles, hurled the man out of his saddle.

As this rider passed him, Marko struck backhanded at the next one. This time, the ax caught the man between neck and shoulder and sank in a hand's breadth. As the man toppled from his seat, Marko wrenched his ax out. He had passed through the line of charging horsemen and made for their chief.

Horses often go in directions other than those wished by their riders. Marko's horse missed the chief, who was also cantering towards him, by a good twelve feet. At that distance, they could only flourish their weapons at each other.

The other riders either had not realized that Marko had cut his way through their line or were unable to turn their mounts to come to their leader's rescue. They cantered away from Marko and the chief for another hundred feet before they began to pull up and turn.

Marko reined his horse into a tight circle. The chief did the same, and this time they came knee to knee.

Clang-cling! went the curved sword of Zaki Riadhi against Marko's buckler, and clang! went Marko's ax against the chief's shield, which like Marko's was of sheet steel. Marko struck again at Zaki's head, covered by a barbute that came down low and almost entirely concealed the robber's features. Zaki caught the blow on his shield again. Although the ax was driven with enough force to break a man's arm, Zaki held his buckler at such an angle that Marko's blow hit it slantwise. The ax twisted out of Marko's hand. He thought for a horrible moment that he had lost it, but the thong around his wrist held it.

Then a plunge of the horses carried the fighters apart, so that Zaki Riadhi's next blow cut empty air. Marko turned his horse again and found himself directly in front of Zaki Riadhi just as his groping fingers got a grip on his ax handle.

Unable to reach the rider, Marko struck at the horse and felt his blade bite into the fine animal's forehead. This was not an honorable blow, but Marko had no time for scruples. The horse fell dead, pitching Zaki Riadhi over its head, almost against Marko's off leg.

Marko brought his ax down once more on the back of the falling chief's helmet. The ax sheared through helmet and skull. The helmet flew off, revealing Zaki's dark, hawk-nosed features. Zaki fell in a heap upon his horse's head. Blood and brains were spattered across the sand.

In the ten seconds that it had taken Marko to kill the leader of the robbers, the others who had ridden at him had turned their horses around and started back. When Marko faced towards his camels, which were now several hundred paces off, the bandits were in front of him and on both sides. They had not yet had time to close in.

"Out of the way!" roared Marko. He raised his ax, still

dripping Zaki's brains, dug the shovel-stirrups into his horse's flanks, and plunged forward.

The Arabis gave way before him, circling and yelping but not quite daring to close with a man twice their size, who had stretched three of their number dead on the sand in half a minute. Marko rode through them and off across the Saar after Halran and the camels.

～ V ～

When Marko caught up with Boert Halran, the Oasis of Siwa was but a smudge of green in the distance. A few robbers had ridden after him, but then they all went back towards the oasis. Marko surmised that they feared to miss the division of the loot and the selection of a new chief. Boert Halran called down:

"I am overjoyed to see you, Marko. For a moment, I

believed they had slain you and that you were one of them pursuing me. Now let us get organized. Which way shall we proceed?"

Marko said: "If we go west, we're bound to reach the Medranian in a few days. We shall then at least be fixed for water. So turn your beasts to the left."

"What shall we do for water meanwhile?"

"Watch for green spots indicating water holes. If we find none, we may be in trouble. Also, there's a spiny plant with thick leaves. When you cut off the spines, you can get moisture from the leaves."

Halran said: "Slim Qadir told me camels can endure several days without water."

"We're not camels. People like Slim know where all the oases are. They leap from one to the next like a man crossing a sea from island to island."

"That was a noteworthy feat, Marko. I never expected a schoolteacher to be so handy with weapons. One—two—three—and three Arabistanis lying dead."

Marko made a deprecatory gesture and looked away with an embarrassed grin. "That was nothing. I'm so much bigger than they that it was like swatting spider-bugs."

"Still, I think you were the only man in the caravan actually to send any of them to Earth."

Marko shrugged. "More luck than skill. If Slim had had his archers under control, those robbers would never have attacked. They fight for loot, not for honor, and they hold off if they think there's any serious risk."

They pulled out the arrow that had struck the riding camel and jogged on. In midafternoon the sunlight be-

The Great Fetish

came uncomfortably warm, so they shed their jackets. Marko's horse began to droop, stumbling along with hanging head, until Marko gave him a rest and asked Halran to change places with him.

"These little Arabistani rabbits aren't built for a man of my size," he said.

With the setting of Muphrid, the moons Gallio and Kopern appeared. Arcturus rose. Swiftly, the temperature fell. Marko made camp. He was handier in such matters than his companion, who was given to absent-minded streaks.

Marko was sweeping the camping area to drive out the bloodsucking arachnids when he looked at Halran. He shouted, "Hey!" and grabbed his companion's arm.

"What?" said Halran.

"I thought you knew those were poison!"

"Oh." Halran dropped the onion-mushroom from which he had been about to take a bite. "I do recall Slim's saying something . . ."

"Well, recall a little sooner next time!"

"Oh, go to space!" said Halran.

The next day, they plodded westward without sighting water. Vegetation became scarcer, until there was nothing to be seen save occasional small spears of phosphor grass, which the animals would not eat. They also found one of the spiny thick-leaved plants, peeled several leaves, and cut them up into slices to eat despite their bitter taste. But they saw no more of these plants. Other travelers must have swept the country along the caravan route clean of them.

Marko asked Halran: "Doctor, you know the story of

my trial for teaching Descensionism. Which belief do you adhere to?"

"Well, the sciences of life are out of my line, but from what I have heard and read, I should say that the arguments for Descensionism were quite strong. My colleagues have confirmed the evolutionary hypothesis to some extent as regards the non-mammals of Kforri. They have done this by finding fossils, which they have pieced together. In some cases, these do seem to be the more primitive ancestors of forms now living. But no such fossils have been found for mammals, including men. Of course, that may be merely the result of mammals being more intelligent and so not getting caught in swamps and similar places where they are likely to be fossilized."

"The question is not really settled, then?"

"Not in the sense that the sphericity of Kforri may be taken as settled, although I think the odds are at least ten to one in favor of Descensionism."

"Then who were the Ancient Ones?"

Halran shrugged. "There are as many interpretations of those myths as there are mythographers. One plausible interpretation is that they were the leaders of a band of settlers who somehow came from Earth and who died or were killed off after the landing. Do you know the story of Hasn the Smith, who, denied an honorable place at the Feast of the Ancient Ones, stood in the doorway and slew them all with his magical arrows?"

"Yes."

"That no doubt refers to some real event, although we do not know what."

Marko asked: "How about the myths of the gods on

Earth, such as the one about the rivalry of the sea god Nelson and the war god Napoleon for the favor of the love goddess Cleopatra?"

"I do not know, though there are the usual speculations. There is a story that the key to these mysteries lies on the Isle of Mnaenn, but the witches do not let outsiders go poking around their sacred island."

The following day, there was still no sign of water. Suffering from thirst, Marko watched for the main caravan route. When he failed to sight it, he could only suppose that they had crossed it without noticing it. It had no permanent marking, and a good breeze soon obliterated the tracks of the animals with blown sand. Halran complained incessantly. Marko twice lost his temper and roared at the older man, feeling ashamed of himself afterwards.

The next day, Halran began to reel in his saddle. They choked down their food as best they could. Marko, rolling a pebble about his mouth to lessen his thirst, looked longingly at a distant herd of dromsors. If he could kill one, its blood would relieve their thirst. But he had no more arrows, and the beasts could easily outrun even a fresh horse.

The day after that, Marko was nodding, half-asleep atop his camel, when a violent jerk of the saddle caused him to open his bloodshot eyes. He blinked, then croaked down to Halran:

"Look! Water! The sea!"

Halran looked. "Huh? Where?"

"There! I suppose you can't see it because I'm higher than you."

Halran wiped his glasses. "Curse my weak eyesight."

Marko shaded his eyes as he gazed towards the faint line of blue, which showed along the horizon between the humps in the barren gray and buff landscape. The animals' nostrils dilated, and their pace quickened.

As he neared the sea, Marko saw that the Saar extended out to the edge of a slope, which ran gently down to a sandy beach. Before he reached the beach, however, a small bay appeared on his right. He angled towards it. The basin in which the bay lay supported a sparse growth of onion-mushrooms and bat-veiled fungi, in contrast to the almost complete lifelessness of the Saar during the last day's ride.

The margins of the bay, however, did not form a beach. A mat of seaweedlike vines made a green strip ten to twenty paces wide around the marge, converting it into a kind of swamp.

Halran kicked and beat the horse into a semblance of a trot. When he reached the vines, he turned left and rode parallel with the shoreline, until he came to where the vine thinned out. Then he flung himself off his mount and ran to the edge of the water, stepping over the few vines.

The horse followed. Sap-sucking arachnids, like large land crabs covered with long red hair, scuttled rustling away. The horse buried its muzzle in the water and drank noisily, while Halran flopped on his belly beside it to drink too.

The camels also showed signs of eagerness. Marko hit Mutasim over the head with the butt of his whip to quiet him and clucked to him to kneel.

When the camels had both knelt, Marko got off. He set

about staking down Mutasim's halter to keep the animal from running away, keeping a wary eye on the creature's head lest it bite him. Then a yell from Boert Halran attracted his attention.

The philosopher was wrestling with a length of acceleratum vine. While he had been drinking, a tendril of the vine, half buried in the sand, had looped itself about one of his legs and had begun to root through the boot. In thrashing about, he had touched another tendril with his arm; this seized him too. He shrieked as the rootlets penetrated his skin.

Marko caught Halran's free hand and tugged, but the effort merely pulled lengths of the vine out of the sand for a few feet until the really thick trunks were exposed, without breaking the hold of the tendrils. Another tendril fastened itself to Halran's other leg. Halran yelled:

"You are pulling my arm off!"

Marko relaxed his grip and got out his ax. Three slashes chopped off the tendrils that had fastened to Halran. The stumps, dripping greenish-white fluid, fell to the ground and lay limply, looking like ordinary harmless vines.

Halran staggered back from the margin of the bay and sat down to cut loose the tendrils still clinging to his arm and legs. First the main tendril had to be cut loose from the rootlets that it had sent through his clothing. Then he had to work off his boots and jacket, leaving the rootlets in his skin. Finally the rootlets had to be pulled out one by one, each leaving a puckery little hole, which bled freely.

"I am a dead man!" said Halran. "I shall bleed to death, or at least be rendered unable to travel!"

"It doesn't look that serious," said Marko. "I had heard of this stuff, but had never seen it. I didn't believe it would root so fast."

"I knew about it," said Halran, "but I erroneously supposed there was not enough at this spot to be dangerous. Or perhaps I was so thirsty I did not think. I am no good at roughing it, no good whatever. There is one individual who got captured." He pointed westward along the shore of the bay to the bones of a dromsor, lying scattered among the cables of the vine.

When he saw that Halran was all right save for minor punctures, Marko walked over to where Halran had been drinking. He severed all the vines that he could see with his ax and kicked the sand to uncover any others beneath the surface. Then he drank, making a face at the taste of the water. Drinking sea water on Kforri might not kill a man, but too much of it would upset his digestion.

After that, Marko led the camels down through the path that he had cut so that they could drink. Halran chased the horse, which had run away when he dropped its reins. The beast was, however, so exhausted that it did not try very hard to escape.

When they were eating, Halran said: "You are an odd fellow, Marko. You have saved my life twice on this trip, yet you have no more compunction about slicing off the head of this fellow who eloped with your wife, and hers too, than you would have about killing one of those." He pointed to one of the hairy arachnids.

"I see nothing odd about it," said Marko. "You're my friend, while Mongamri wronged me in a malevolent and perfidious manner. So it's only right that I should kill him. But I agreed to drop the plan out of deference to you."

"So you did, so you did. I had forgotten."

⁂

They marched north along the eastern shore of the Medranian Sea, sometimes seeing the white tooth of a sail or the black plume of a steamer's smoke on the horizon. One of Marko's burning ambitions was to ride a steamship, despite the fact that their bronzen boilers sometimes blew up with grisly results. But then, Halran explained, they had been invented only a half century earlier and were not yet perfected. During his sabbatical, Marko had admired a couple of the craft tied up to the piers at Chef. He would have liked to go aboard to look around, but his timid shyness had prevented his asking permission.

Marko continued to ply Halran with questions, partly because it seemed like a good opportunity to enlarge his knowledge and partly to practice his Anglonian. The only trouble was that, once opened up, Halran talked so much that Marko got little chance to speak any language.

The day after they reached the seashore, they picked up the main caravan trail. They were running low on food. That presented no pressing difficulty, because the onion-mushrooms here were edible. One could live for a while on these. To go for long without other foods, however, caused tooth decay and other ills.

They also encountered a couple of caravans headed the other way. Each time, the people were so interested in the story of Zaki Riadhi's raid that they entertained

Marko and Halran with all the food and drink they could hold.

As they turned the northeast corner of the Medranian Sea, the terrain became greener. Sometimes there was a spatter of rain. Cultivation appeared, then villages inhabited by folk of mixed Arabi-Anglonian descent. They crossed the guarded border from Arabistan into the Republic of Anglonia. Marko had worried about his lack of passport, which he knew to be needed in Anglonia and Eropia. But Halran assured him that he could get him in on his own, by a simple endorsement, as his assistant. So it proved.

Marko knew little of Anglonia, save what the Vizantian geography textbooks said: "... mostly flat, but hilly in the northern parts ... the people are friendly and gay, but shameless, frivolous, and unreliable ... their children are spoiled ... the principal exports are wheat, bron fiber, iron ore, pure-bred livestock, and ingenious mechanical devices. ..." Therefore he looked about him with interest.

The Anglonians, he found, were a tall, handsome people. Many had blond hair and blue eyes. They also had a widespread tendency towards obesity. Most of them over twenty (Kforrian years) were fat and paunchy.

They did not seem exactly frivolous. At least they were not lazy. They worked and played with furious intensity. They loved speed, and their light carriages tore through crowded towns at full gallop. They were not merely friendly; they were impudently and insatiably curious. Every time Marko and Halran sat down in an eating place, the Anglonians crowded around, introducing themselves. They asked the details of Marko's past history, present occupation, and future prospects. They asked about his love life until he turned purple with embarrassment and pretended not to understand them.

When the Anglonians were not inquiring, they talked about themselves. Marko had never met such garrulous people. As far as he could tell, their main topics were food and sex, mostly loud boasts of their own prowess in both lines. Both sexes dressed gaudily, used perfume, and were given to public drunkenness and quarreling. Thinking them decadent, Marko at times preferred the dour dignity and cold reserve of his native land.

Halran suggested that Marko could avoid this friendly persecution by looking more like an Anglonian. Accordingly, Marko bought a pair of knitted trunk-hose like those of his comrade and retired his baggy trousers to his bag. The new pants embarrassed him by their tightness, but the Anglonians paid less attention to him. He kept his boots, because he was used to them. Anyway, they looked much like Anglonian riding boots.

The hair had grown on Marko's scalp and jaw during his journey. Instead of having his pate shaven but for the scalp lock, he had that lock cut off and left the rest as it was, in a short blond bristle like that of the Anglonians. He also began cultivating one of the mustaches affected by these folk. He bought a tobacco pipe and learned, with much coughing and spitting, to smoke it, instead of chewing plug like a Vizantian.

On the fourteenth of Newton, they stopped at an eating place in Kambra. Marko was just getting well into his meal when Halran squeezed his wrist and said:

"Do not look around, Marko, but get ready to pay your bill and go."

"Huh?"

"Do as I say. I shall explain subsequently."

Grumbling, Marko did as he was told. When they were on the road again, he asked Halran what had happened. Halran said:

"Did you not notice that trio of youths at the bar, staring at us?"

"I did in a vague sort of way. Why?"

"I could tell by their actions they were contemplating an assault upon us."

"Oh? If they had, I should have simply knocked their heads together hard enough to crack them."

"That is what I feared. If, in defending us, you had injured one of them, we should have at least been mobbed. If we survived, the law would have dealt severely with us."

"Napoin! Why?"

"They were *minors*, and nobody is allowed to injure a minor in Anglonia."

"So what?" snorted Marko. "All the more reason to knock their heads together, to teach them respect for their elders."

"Do not let anybody hear you say that. Minors are sacred in Anglonia. They are not held responsible for their actions, but any harm done them is severely punished."

"Sometimes," said Marko, "Anglonians almost act like reasonable people, and at others like a race of lunatics. What's the reasoning behind this worship of minors?"

"Why, you see, we believe that if a child or young person is thwarted or curbed in any way, he will grow up into a sour, frustrated, mentally diseased adult. So they are allowed to do pretty much as they please, on the theory that they will thus work off all their antisocial impulses before reaching their majority. That is why all adult Anglonians are so well adjusted."

Marko spat in the dust.

On the eighteenth of Newton, Marko and his companion came to the seaport of Niok, which rose in graceful spires and crude blocks from the estuary of the Mizzipa River.

VI

When Marko Prokopiu and Boert Halran got to Niok, Marko wanted to stop a few days to make sure that his intended victims were not there. Halran was anxious to push on to Lann, in order to complete his aerostatic experiment in time for the philosophers' convention. They agreed to split up. Halran kept the horse and the burden camel, paying Marko half the estimated value of the horse. He said:

"Good-bye, then. If you get to Lann, come and visit me."

"I will, sir," said Marko.

Halran rode off towing his burden camel, still swaying under the four great jars of stupa gum. Marko spent the rest of the day in the stock market. Thinking himself a poor bargainer, he was sure that the more worldly-wise Halran would have obtained a better deal.

Actually, Marko was not so bad as he thought. His embarrassment over haggling caused him to put on a stiff, stony air. This, together with his monstrous brawn, gave traders the impression that he was more self-assured than he was. Eventually he traded the camel for a large horse and a few extra dlars.

He spent the next two days searching for Mongamri and his wife. The search took him through Niok's endless rows of drink shops, brothels, and the dives of marwan addicts. Sometimes rough-looking characters stared threateningly or muttered at him, but they turned away on noting his ax and musculature.

Niokers, he found, were an even noisier species than ordinary Anglonians, much given to outbursts of rage over trivial matters. They would leap up and down like tersors on perches and scream threats and insults. The minute Marko put on his fighting face and reached for his ax, however, they found reason to go elsewhere.

A suspicious, discourteous, and truculent race with no sense of dignity, Marko thought. He was puzzled by their common expletive *"Cop!"* (pronounced something like "kyop" or "chop") until he realized that it was the shrunken remnant, in Niokese dialect, of the name of the goddess of love, Cleopatra, or as Vizantians pronounced it "Kliopat." Also, despite the alleged sanctity of human life in Anglonia, he got used to the sight of the bodies of murdered men in the gutters.

On the other hand, the Niokers were perfectly willing, if Marko acted friendly towards them, to suggest a joint foray into vice or crime. It was, he supposed, their notion of doing a stranger a good turn.

Marko had given much thought to the handling of Mongamri and Petronela. While he was not sure that he had done right in promising Halran not to kill them, he could not go back on his promise without feeling even guiltier than he did over sparing them. Vizantians took the keeping of one's word with as much seriousness as they did sexual morality. And there was something to the maxim "When in Roum, behave as do the Roumians."

The idea of copying the loose morals of the Anglonians had a certain sinister appeal to Marko. But, brought up where such matters were surrounded by a high wall of puritanical inhibitions, he could no more have advanced an improper proposal to a woman than he could have walked on the Medranian Sea. The mere thought of exposing himself to rebuff and embarrassment gave him cold chills.

§§§

Marko jogged into Lann, a sprawling old city built of the dark-gray limestone of that region. When he had taken quarters, he set out through the narrow, crooked streets to find Mongamri.

First he went to the public library. By asking for Mongamri's books, he learned the names of his publishers. He found that he could understand literate Lanners well enough, although the slurred, whining dialect of the working class defeated him.

Then he found where these people did business. This was a matter of some difficulty, because the Lanners had no rational system of naming or numbering their streets. One thoroughfare might have five different names in the course of ten blocks.

Marko called at the office of the first publisher on his list and asked where Mongamri lived. He presented himself as a friend whom Mongamri had met in his travels. The publisher gave the address with what seemed to Marko a rash lack of suspicion. In Vizantia one was chary of giving out such information, because the seeker might be a feudist out to kill a member of a hostile family.

He returned to his quarters for siesta. Afterwards he got detailed directions to get to Mongamri's address and drew a sketch map. Since the place was well out in the suburbs, he rode his horse out to Mongamri's house.

The house was smaller and less impressive than Marko had expected. He had a vague idea that an Anglonian literary man would live in the style of a Vizantian magnate. Here, the address turned out to be a little fieldstone bungalow in a medium-poor neighborhood.

Marko still had not finally decided just what to do with these people. He would not kill them save in self-defense, but he owed it to his self-respect to give the faithless Chet the beating of a lifetime. As for Petronela . . . If she were willing to come back to him, that might be worked out for as long as he stayed in Anglonia. But he could not take her back to Vizantia, as his disgraceful failure to slay her would then be patent to all. Of course, he might never go back to Vizantia. . . .

Marko opened the flap of his ax sheath and reached for the door knocker. It took all his self-mastery to force himself to bang the knocker. What should he say if . . .

The door opened. There stood Petronela, tall and big-boned, looking like any other young Anglonian housewife. Marko felt a boil of conflicting emotions rising within him.

Petronela recognized Marko despite the budding mustache. She screamed and tried to slam the door, but Marko had thrust his boot into the crack.

Petronela let go the door and ran back into the house. Marko followed, surmising that she would lead him to Mongamri.

"Chet!" shrieked Petronela in Anglonian. "He's here!"

She led Marko into a room at the back. Mongamri sat at a desk littered with papers and cigarette butts, correcting a set of proof sheets. When Marko shouldered his way into the room, Mongamri said:

"*Kyopt!* You, eh?"

Marko began in a coldly cutting tone: "Yes, you swine, it's I. Perhaps you'd be so good as to explain—"

Mongamri picked up a large Arabistani knife, which he kept on his desk as a paperweight and letter opener. He lunged towards Marko, raising his arm for a stab.

Marko threw up his left arm. The point of the knife pierced skin and flesh and stuck into the bone, while with his right hand Marko fumbled for his ax. Although he had not meant to kill Mongamri, this attack altered matters.

As Mongamri drew back the dagger for another stab, Marko got his ax out. Lacking room to swing, he thrust the spike on the end into Mongamri's chest and gave a push that hurled Mongamri across the room.

Mongamri fell back against his desk, knocking a lamp off with a crash. Marko stood where he was, ax half raised. Mongamri slipped down until he was sitting on the floor with his back to the desk. He muttered something in which Marko heard the word "police," fell over sideways, and lay still.

"You killed him!" cried Petronela. She glanced at the ax, which Marko had lowered so that blood dripped from the spike, and darted to the door.

"Petronela," said Marko, "if you'll promise—"

"I'll see you hanged!" screamed Petronela, and fled.

"Hey!" called Marko. "I didn't intend . . . If you will . . ."

The front door slammed. Marko hurried after Petronela, sure that, if he stayed where he was, he would soon find himself involved with the unknown laws of this strange land.

When he looked out the front door, there was no sign of Petronela. He paused to think out a plan. Then he stepped back into Mongamri's study to see if Mongamri were truly dead. (He was.) Marko went out, mounted, and rode briskly back to his lodging. There he bandaged his slight wound, paid his rent, gathered up his gear, and moved out. He rode to the house of Boert Halran.

§§§

"Oh, very well, very well," said Halran, wrinkling his nose. "After all, you did save my life. According to your story, you acted in self-defense. So you may hide out here. But if anybody inquires, you told me nothing of your escapade, do you understand?"

"I understand, sir," said Marko, staring at the floor and flushing. "I'll try to be as little trouble as possible."

"I warned you something of that sort would happen. Oho!" said Halran, looking at Marko with bright piercing eyes. "That gives me an idea. When I got home I found that my apprentice, curse him, had gone away and refuses to return."

"Can't you have him flogged back?" said Marko.

"Not in Anglonia. It occurs to me, however, that you might have difficulty in making your exit from Lann in the usual manner, if the police are watching for you. I doubt if you are rich enough to obtain release by bribery in the event of your capture."

"What then?" said Marko.

"Be my new assistant! You will pass out of Lann through the air where nobody can seize you."

"What, me fly in your machine?" cried Marko.

"Certainly. Are you afraid?"

"A Skudran afraid? No, but the idea startled me. Are you sure I'm not too heavy?"

"No. The balloon was designed to carry my apprentice and me, and he was even heavier than you."

Marko almost asked if Halran would pay him. But he remembered that, as a fugitive, he was already asking all that he decently could. He said:

"May I see the balloon now?"

"Come this way."

Halran led Marko out the back of his house. His yard overflowed with a huge, shapeless mass of cloth, sewn together in contrasting strips of black and white. Clustered around the mass were a score of women of all ages, brushing on the stupa gum that Halran had brought from Vizantia. They chattered like a flock of tersors as they heaved the heavy folds this way and that in order to get the gum on every square inch.

"Come and meet my family," said Boert Halran. "Dorthi, this is Marko Prokopiu, my new assistant. Marko, my wife, and these are my daughters Bitris, Viki, Greta, and Henrit."

Marko acknowledged the introductions with the formal manners drilled into him years before. Halran said:

"The other women are housewives of Lann, mostly my wife's brizh-playing friends. I got them *organized*." He grinned like an imp and launched into a lecture on aerostatics, pacing about and gesturing to indicate mathematical concepts.

VII

Six days later, on the fifth of Perikles, the gum had dried and the balloon was ready. Boert Halran said:

"I will send one of my daughters to make the rounds of the newspapers, asking each to send a reporter to witness this great event."

"Hey!" said Marko. "If they see me . . ."

"Oh. I forgot. Couldn't you wear a mask?"

Marko shook his head. "That would whet their suspicions."

Halran sighed. "Very well. I need publicity to elicit more financial support, though; these experiments are fiendishly expensive. But we shall hope the sight of our soaring over the rooftops of Lann will furnish adequate excitement. I will send Viki merely to get the weather report. Not that it will help much; old Ronni is right about as often as if he stayed indoors and guessed."

As Muphrid set, little Viki Halran returned with the report that there was no indication of a disturbance in the northeast tradewinds. Marko had been casting an eye with a little more than purely academic interest on Halran's four daughters. (A fifth, married, lived in Niok.) All were handsome, vivacious girls. He did not, however, go beyond looking. Besides the puritanism of his culture and his own introversion, he was inhibited by his inner turmoil about Petronela.

As for the girls, Marko thought that they regarded him as an amiable and amusing monster. All four girls had suitors of their own.

Marko had been horrified the first time one of these youths had called for an evening and paid his respects (in a casual and impudent manner) to the older Halrans. Then he and the girl had retired to a bedroom, whence soon came audible creakings.

Marko's overthrow was complete the next evening. The four girls quarreled shrilly over the fact that each had a lover and there were not enough bedrooms to go around. Viki broke the deadlock by asking Marko if he would lend his cot in the attic. Marko, red to the ears, could only gulp and nod.

"If it will inconvenience you," said Viki, evidently mistaking his silence for unwillingness, "I can repay you by—"

"N-no, no, do not of it think," said Marko in his broken Anglonian. "I only too happy am."

"Oh? If you hesitate on account of your wife, Petronela, she isn't your wife anymore anyway."

"No?"

"No. My sister Henrit saw the notice of divorce in yesterday's paper. We meant to tell you, but such a little thing slipped our minds. So now you're fair game for all of us."

"Thank you. I am being much interested." Marko bowed formally.

During the next few days, Marko thought he had been a fool not at least to have found out what Viki was offering. A man, once womaned but now womanless, finds celibacy much harder to bear than one who has never known a woman at all. Marko had now been unwomaned long enough so that the primal urge drove him nearly crazy.

To the Halran family, however, he presented an effect of urbane dignity and good humor. He struggled to improve his command of the language and kept his eyes open for the minutiae of Anglonian manners. Inside, he was a mass of conflicting emotions.

※ ※ ※

When he got word that the good weather would hold, Boert Halran ordered Marko and his family to rig the balloon for inflation. The three moons were sweeping through the dark sky when they finished this onerous task. Halran lit the fire in the main peat stove.

"I hoped to get off several days earlier," he explained to Marko. "This is the beginning of the hurricane season. But I think we shall make out all right, and that we shall arrive at the convention in ample time for the opening."

It took all night to inflate the balloon. Marko and Halran took turns feeding the fire and sleeping. When the water clock indicated an hour before dawn, the bag of the balloon swayed overhead, holding the ropes taut. Halran explained:

"By filling it at night, one can conserve much ballast. As Muphrid strikes the bag, it warms the air and imparts extra lift to it. Are you ready?"

They placed in the basket the equipment that they were taking, including Marko's ax but not, for weight, his shield. Marko climbed up the ropes to the small stove above the basket and got that fire going, too. Halran's women smothered him with embraces, and the girls made plain their intention of kissing Marko, too. Marko had been shocked with the freedom with which people kissed in public in Anglonia. By now, however, he was so hardened to these people's loose ways that he even enjoyed the transaction.

Marko and Boert Halran climbed into the basket, cast off, and waved good-bye. Marko's heart rose into his throat as the dark ground dropped away and the lights of Lann appeared below him. People were already abroad.

Marko thought that the ascent might be unnoticed, as the sky had not yet begun to pale. But the glow of the little stove overhead soon attracted attention. People shouted, ran, and looked up, pointing.

The swift rise of the balloon, however, soon caused the clamoring voices to fade. After the first few minutes, Marko could no longer gage their rate of ascent. As they rose, their horizontal movement speeded up also. Soon, the lights of Lann slid out from under them to the northeast. The temperature fell until Marko put on his sheepskin.

"If my calculations are correct," said Halran, "the wind ought to drop us down within a few miles of Vien by this time tomorrow."

"I hope you're right," said Marko.

For the first hour or two, nothing happened. Muphrid rose through banded streaks of cloud, which soon thickened to hide it in a high overcast. Marko and Halran ate. Between intervals of climbing up the ropes to tuck another briquette of peat into the stove, Marko hung over the edge of the basket, gazing down upon toylike houses and farms.

"Now remember," said Halran, "when we touch down, stand by to pull the rip cord just a second before the basket touches, or we shall be dragged and spilled out. I shall give you the signal."

The rip cord, Marko knew, opened a great slit in the upper part of the balloon by pulling down the slide of a zip fastener. The garrulous little philosopher went on:

"I sent messages to my colleagues in Vien asking for a proclamation that, if a great bag came down out of sky with a man dangling under it in a basket, it was a harmless scientific experiment and not a visitation from

Earth. When I made my first trial flight, I descended on a farm in the vicinity of Lann. The peasants thought I was a devil and would have killed me with pitchforks if I had not taken flight. They tore my balloon to fragments, too."

He fussed about the basket, checking his altitude by a sighting device with cross wires. Once he dropped the sand from a ballast bag and told Marko to stoke up the peat fire. Then they went up too fast, and Halran had to valve air to bring them down again.

As time drifted silently by, little dark-gray clouds appeared below and on a level with them. At first they were so small and few as hardly to be noticed, but Halran muttered:

"I do not like that. Curse it, if I could only check our direction by Muphrid!"

The high overcast had become so thick that no trace of sun could be seen. The little clouds multiplied and grew, until the balloon seemed to be drifting in the midst of a great throng of them. Now and then a flash of lightning lit them up, and thunder rolled in the distance. Marko realized that they were drifting in the midst of a great storm. Because the balloon went with the wind, there was no feeling of motion or rush of wind.

The balloon, however, became hard to control. It either shot up until Halran had to valve air or dropped until he had to drop ballast, while Marko stoked the fire. Marko understood that, when they ran out of either ballast or peat, they would soon have to come down.

On one descent, they plunged into a mass of cloud. The mist around them got darker and darker. Marko wondered what that pattering noise was, until he realized that rain was striking the gas bag. The cooling effect of the rain made the balloon drop faster than ever, until they broke out of the bottom of the layer of cloud.

Marko was astonished to see the ground a mere seventy-five feet below, shooting past at a dizzy speed. Below them, plants bent in the wind, which roared as it poured over the ground. The rain was coming down hard, but the bag of the balloon acted as an umbrella. Marko could not tell which way they were going, because the whole balloon was spinning round and round, so that the landscape spun in the opposite direction below. He glimpsed an Anglonian cowboy in a broad-brimmed hat, chivying a small herd of cattle into an enclosure.

Halran yelled at him, then pulled the drop strings on three bags of ballast. Up they went again, this time so fast that Marko was conscious of the wind's downward rush. After an endless time of seeing nothing but lurid lightning flashes and being deafened by thunder, they broke out the top again, not far below the upper overcast. Below them, Marko saw a solid mass of blackish clouds boiling like one of the volcanic hot swamps of northern Vizantia.

"We had better remain up here," said Halran. "Curse it, if I only knew my direction . . ."

By rapid stoking, they stayed safely above the storm for the next few hours. They ate. Marko shivered with cold. Halran checked his remaining supplies of fuel and sand. He clucked apprehensively, glanced over the side, and squawked like a marsh tersor.

"Look!" he yelled, pointing downward.

Marko saw, through a rift in the clouds, the crawling, wrinkled surface of the Medranian Sea.

VIII

Hours passed. The clouds began to break up, both above and below the balloon. The setting Muphrid shot golden lances through the gaps, gliding the bag of the balloon as well as the underside of the overcast. Marko, looking down upon the leaden sea, cried:

"Dr. Halran! An island!"

Halran looked. In the crawling waste of waters, half

hidden by fracted scud clouds, a darker mass appeared ahead.

Halran, frowning over his homemade chart, said: "A large one, Marko. I think the wind will carry us over it."

"Shall we land there?"

"We shall have to. Otherwise this storm will carry us far over the sea, and when we run out of peat we shall have to descend willy-nilly. The only thing that concerns me is the reception we shall receive."

"Why," said Marko, "there's nothing to fear from a handful of fishermen."

"If I am not in error, that is the Isle of Mnaenn."

"You mean the one with the witches?"

"That is what they are called, though what they really are like I cannot say. The only visitors they allow are those who come to practice oneiromancy in their Temple of Einstein and to purchase spells and potions."

"What is oneiromancy?"

"Divination by dreams. You sleep in the temple and next day tell the witches your dream to interpret."

"Do you believe in that sort of thing, Doctor?"

"I think it is superstitious nonsense, but I could be mistaken. There is much about which we cannot issue definitive dicta. Of course, some of the witches' customers are attracted less by the witches' alleged magical powers than by the fact that they include as part of their fee that the visitor shall be intimate with them."

"Why do the witches want visitors to be intimate with them?"

"Because it is an all-female society, and that is their only method of maintaining their numbers."

Marko said: "I shouldn't think many visitors would mind. At least, those who weren't from my country, where moral standards are stricter. But why hasn't some neighboring ruler annexed the island? A handful of women couldn't stop a conqueror, even if the girls were armed."

"Ah, but they can. The island is surrounded by tall cliffs, with only one or two landing places. The girls would have ample time to drop boulders on the heads of any invaders."

Marko shaded his eyes and peered towards the land they were nearing. "That's funny."

"What is so risible?"

"I see no cliffs. This island—if it be an island—has broad beaches."

"Oh!" said Halran, peering in his turn. "You are correct, as nearly as my cursed eyesight can make it out. Besides, this island is much too large for Mnaenn."

"What is it, then?"

"Afka, I suppose, unless there are other islands in this part of the Medranian that I know not of. Afka lies south and east of Mnaenn. Good gods, we must have flown right over Mnaenn without seeing it!"

"I've heard of Afka but don't know much about it. What's it like? We never go there, because the Afkans are said to be unfriendly to strangers."

Halran shrugged. "Not much more is known in Anglonia. The populace is said to be dark of skin and too proud to mingle with the lesser breeds. Well, we shall soon learn. Get ready to bring us down. I say, what's that?"

"What?"

"It looks like a stupa forest. But we could not possibly have been blown clear to the Borsja Peninsula!"

"Are you sure that is the only place where those big trees grow, Doctor?"

"No one is ever certain, but we shall soon find out. Valve some more air, please."

The balloon settled gently to the mossy ground, between the curving beach and the looming forest. The trees were unmistakable stupas, although but a fraction of the size of those on the Borsja Peninsula. The latter reached a height of a thousand feet. On the other hand, these trees were far larger than the dwarf stupas of the civilized lands.

Marko and Halran were still folding and tying up the bag, when men approached and surrounded them. These were big men, with skins of so dark a brown as to look black. Their kinky black hair was trimmed into fanciful shapes. They carried spears and crossbows. The leader, in a kind of scarlet toga, gestured and spoke threateningly.

After Marko and Halran had tried several languages between them, it was found that one of the spearmen spoke a little Vizantian. With this man as interpreter, the leader conveyed the word that the foreigners were to come with him.

"What about my balloon?" asked Halran.

"You will not long care what happens to it," said he of the toga. "Now march!"

The other black men formed a hollow square around the travelers. They marched in step, keeping rigid formation, to the leader's chant of "*Moja*, mbili, tatu, ine, *moja*, mbili, tatu, ine. . . ."

"What have you gotten us into now?" grumbled Marko.

"Oh, dear, oh, dear! Do not blame me; blame the storm. But I admit I was a fool, not to have landed as soon as the weather got thick. We may be doomed for all I know; these beggars have a bad reputation."

"Well, let's keep our eyes and ears open. Something may come up."

Halran sighed gustily and shook his head. "Ah, me, never to see my dear ones again!" Then he jerked up his head. "By Newton, that's curious!"

"What is?"

They had entered the forest and marched along a straight path. Among the trunks of the stupa trees, on all sides, ran a system of pipes, supported at eye level by posts. From the joints of these pipes, a gentle spray of water moistened the forest floor.

"So that is how they keep their woods from burning up!" said Halran.

"How do you mean?"

"You know, Marko, that the Borsja Peninsula is the only place, so far explored, that produces decent hardwood in quantity. The reason is the extreme dampness, with constant rain and fog. Since forest fires cannot get started, the trees can grow undisturbed for thousands of years—unless some greedy entrepreneur, like your Sokrati Popu, cuts them all down. So these people, finding that they had a good stand of hardwood, have taken measures to protect it, making Afka into a kind of artificial Borsja."

"I can tell you something else," said Marko. "They didn't find these trees here. They planted them."

"Really! How do you know?"

"Look at those even rows! No natural forest ever grew in a formation like that."

Halran wiped his glasses. "By the gods, you are right! With my weak sight, I should never have noticed in this inadequate light. The Afkans must have an advanced technology."

Thereafter, the travelers had to save their breath for walking. Their captors, surrounding them with spears warily leveled, set a brisk pace. Both were weary and footsore when, over an hour later, they came to the end of the forest.

Ahead lay cultivated fields, from which Afkans were on their way home to supper. They marched in gangs, each under control of an overseer with a whistle.

In the twilight, the fields gave way to a perfectly square town. Houses of timber and plaster, of severely plain, square, monotonous design, were set on streets laid in a square grid pattern. An Afkan was lighting lamps at the street corners with a long-handled device.

"Not what one would call charm," said Halran. "It is like an overgrown barracks."

"At least," said Marko, recalling the tangled alleys of Niok and Lann, "it should be easy to find one's way around."

The escort stopped in front of a building, distinguished from the rest only by its greater size. A pair of sentries, armed with swords and crossbows, stood rigidly in front of the entrance. The lamplight gleamed on their polished bronzen cuirasses and helmets.

He of the toga went in. After a long wait, he returned with several others of his kind.

"Follow us," he said through the interpreter.

Inside, the building was bare and functional. The travelers were ushered into a large room. Black men sat impassively in chairs. Marko and Halran remained standing, each with a pair of spearmen to guard him.

For the next hour, the travelers were minutely questioned about their origin, their purpose, and the nature of Halran's flying machine. Their inquisitors at first all looked alike to Marko, the more so since they never allowed a flicker of expression to ruffle their dignity. By and by, however, he began to distinguish them. One man, a little shorter and stouter than the others, seemed to be an object of deference.

Then another black arrived. This was an elderly man in a white toga, with a conical hat on his kinky gray hair. He spoke to the inquisitors and then, in good Anglonian, to the travelers.

"We can dispense with this clumsy interpretation," he said. "I am Ndovu, high priest of Laa. That"—he indicated the stout man—"is Chaka, the Kabaka of Afka. The others are his ministers. I was absent when you arrived but came as soon as I heard. Repeat, briefly, what you have told the Kabaka."

"Please sir, may we sit down?" said Halran. "I am ready to faint with weariness."

Ndovu nodded and spoke to the spearmen, who brought stools. When Halran had been through his tale once again, the high priest said: "It is plausible. You say this flying device is your invention?"

"Yes, sir."

"Hm. It is too bad that we shall have to kill a man of your gifts, Professor."

"*Oy!* What have we done to deserve this fate?"

"You have set foot on the sacred soil of Afka, that is what you have done. For hundreds of years, we have published abroad the fact that we want no contact with outsiders and that any who come here without special authorization are liable to death. You have aggravated your offense by not only coming here but also by inventing a device whereby others could easily do likewise, thus imperiling our isolation."

"Why are you so insistent on your precious isolation?"

"To preserve the purity of our blood. If outsiders were let in, sooner or later one would contract a liaison with one of our women. Our racial integrity would be threatened."

Marko spoke: "How long have we, sir?"

"Until morning. We do things here in proper order, and it will take that long for the courts to process your case. But see here, my man, it is for us to ask questions, not you!"

The high priest spoke to the guards, who began to hustle Marko and Halran out.

"Holy Father!" cried Halran. "At least you owe us—ah —spiritual consolation, don't you?"

As the guards hesitated, the high priest gave a faint smile—the first expression that Marko had yet seen on an Afkan face. "I suppose so. I shall visit you later this evening, after the supper you so inconveniently interrupted."

※※※

When Ndovu came to their cell, he said: "I take it that the true faith of Laa is not known in your barbarous land?"

"Indeed not, sir," said Halran. "Enlighten us, I pray."

"Well, in the beginning Laa created the heavens and the earth. He also created the first man and woman, named Kongo and Kenya respectively.

"For many centuries, the descendants of Kongo and Kenya dwelt happily in the land. Then some of the people fell into sinful ways. I do not have time for all the details, but suffice it to say that Laa cursed these sinful ones by bleaching their skins. Before then, all mankind had been black, like us.

"More time passed. Then the cursed ones, the paleskins, waxed in numbers. By a sudden onset, they overcame the virtuous blackskins and made slaves of them. For many generations, they forced the blackskins to labor at menial tasks.

"At last, Laa sent the captive blackskins a leader, named Mozo, to lead them out of captivity. Mozo warned the king of the paleskins that, unless he let Laa's chosen people go, the king's folk would suffer grievous chastisement.

"But the king did not believe this. He drove Mozo out with scorn and insults. As a result, his folk were afflicted with incursions of transors and other pests, drouth, epidemics, and other misfortunes. After seven of these plagues had befallen the paleskins, their king at last agreed to let Laa's folk go. So they went forth under the guidance of Mozo.

"Then the king repented him of having yielded to Mozo's threats and set out in pursuit with his army. But, when the blackskins came to the shores of the Medranian Sea, Mozo prayed to Laa, who parted the waters of the sea. Thus Laa's folk crossed over to Afka dry-shod. But when the king of the paleskins and his army sought to follow, the waters returned and drowned them all.

"Ere he died, Mozo called his people together and propounded a code of laws for them. Amongst these laws, besides the usual prohibitions of lying, theft, murder, impiety, and so on, he ordained that all Afkans must be efficient, energetic, and industrious. They must arm to the teeth and be ready at all times to defend themselves and the land that Laa had given them.

"The cursed ones had enslaved them, he said, because they had taken life too easily. In enjoying life, they had let the paleskins get ahead of them in organization and technology. This, he said, must never happen again. It is ordained that, the more a man gives up the pleasures of life in this world, the greater shall be his pleasures in Earth."

"You Afkans seem like a grimly puritanical lot," said Halran, "if you will excuse my saying so."

Ndovu beamed. "No apologies needed. What you say is high praise here. Now, Mozo also insisted upon the racial purity of the folk, if they wished Laa to continue to love and protect them. During their time of slavery, there had naturally been some mixture between the two races, so

The Great Fetish

that many blackskins were actually of paler shades. Ever since, if a newborn infant betrays paleskin blood by its color, it is destroyed. Thus we have weeded out nearly all trace of the blood of the cursed ones, and we are determined to maintain this purity at all costs. Now do you understand?"

§-§-§

The cell was clean, but the bars were stout and the lock unpickable, at least with any means the travelers had to hand. The guards in the corridor had no words in common with the prisoners and ignored their efforts at communication. Halran bemoaned his lot.

After a restless night, Marko and Halran were led out at sunrise, with their wrists tied behind them. At the scaffold, they found High Priest Ndovu awaiting them.

"I thought that such gifted outsiders as yourselves deserved spiritual consolation at the highest level," he said. "Let us join in a prayer to Laa, the merciful, the compassionate."

During the prayer, the executioner kept testing the edge of his ax with his thumb. Halran's teeth chattered audibly. Marko miserably felt that there was something he could say that would avert their fate, only he could not quite think what it was. Ndovu droned:

". . . and so, as your heads fall, may your souls fly to the realms above with the speed of a bolt from a crossbow—"

"Sir!" cried Marko. "Listen to me!"

"Yes, my son?"

"Look, you hold it against us for inventing the balloon, don't you?"

"Yes. I explained that."

"Well, if we invented something that would help you to keep outsiders away, wouldn't that make up for it?"

"Hm," said Ndovu. "What have you in mind?"

"If it works, will you let us go?"

"I cannot promise that; the cabinet and the supreme court would have to concur."

"Well, ask them."

The executioner spoke. "Holy Father, I cannot stand around all morning. I have my orders."

Ndovu said: "Well, I will grant you a one-day reprieve on my own authority; we are a just people. But this had better not be a ruse, merely to gain a few days of life." He spoke to the guards, who led Marko and Halran back to their cell.

When they were alone again, Halran said: "What is this, Marko? I hope you were not merely bluffing. If you were, they may find some more lingering finish for us."

"I hope I wasn't, either. It was that last remark of his, about crossbow bolts."

"Well?"

"These people have the crossbow, just as ours do. It struck me that, if we could make an oversized crossbow, mounted on some sort of frame or pedestal, it could shoot bolts the size of spears, and much farther than any ordinary missile weapon."

"What were the purpose? These folk seem militaristic enough without our adding to their arsenal."

"Some of these supercrossbows, mounted around the

coasts of this island, should discourage unwanted visitors."

Halran mused: "I seem to remember something in the old literature about such a device. It was called a 'gun' or a 'catapult.' As I remember, however, it discharged with a flash and a clap of thunder and hurled a ball of metal."

"We have none of these legendary weapons, but the Afkans have plenty of good, strong wood to make a big crossbow from."

※※※

So it came to pass that, a few days later, Marko Prokopiu and Boert Halran stood again on the northern shore of Afka, watching a squad of Afkan soldiers inflate their balloon. The high priest said:

"I should have liked you to remain until your shooter was completed and tested. I have enjoyed our conversations and the news you have brought of the outside world. Luckily, I am deemed holy enough"—Ndovu smiled faintly—"not to have my soul endangered by intercourse with cursed ones."

"Thank you, Holy Father," said Halran.

Ndovu continued: "Colonel Mkubwa is sure that, having grasped the principle of your device, he can, with the help of our skilled craftsmen, complete it himself. The Kabaka is anxious to get you off our sacred soil, lest you steal out and impregnate our women. It is a common belief that all paleskins are superhumanly lusty and incorrigibly lecherous."

"Now it is you who flatter us," said Halran.

When the balloon was filled, and Marko and Halran

climbed into the basket, the high priest called out: "Laa be with you!" and waved. The mild southeast breeze carried the balloonists off Afka in the direction of Lann. Halran said:

"I have never been strong for priests; but, of the Afkans, Ndovu seemed the most human of the lot. It would not do to tell him so, though. He wouldn't take it as a compliment."

IX

Marko said: "Damn it, Boert, can't you learned men do something about the speed of the wind? Last time, it got us in trouble by blowing twice as fast as expected. This time it bids fair to do the same by blowing only half as fast."

Muphrid lay low on the western horizon. Ahead, already in shadow, lay the island of Mnaenn.

Halran sighed and shrugged. "At this rate, the convention will be half over before we can get there. We have a choice of either descending on Mnaenn, or continuing on northwestward and alighting in the sea when our fuel and ballast give out, some time tonight. Would you prefer the latter?"

Marko sighed in his turn. "I suppose not. The witches will probably want to kill us, too, as the Afkans did. They may have something more refined and lingering than a quick chop."

"We talked our way out of the last one," said Halran. "It is not inconceivable that we can do the same with this."

"Yes? You know the old saw about taking a jug to the fountain one time too many. I don't get inspirations like that often."

"We do what we can, not what we would." Halran busied himself with the valve cord. Marko heard the hiss of escaping air. The balloon sank.

The last rays of Muphrid turned scarlet, then purple, as the island waxed before them. The horizon rose to occlude the disk of the luminary.

Towards the center of the island, a group of structures came into view in the twilight. Dominating the group was a domed building of sacerdotal monumentality. Around the houses stretched the plateau, an irregular surface broken by a few dwarf stupas, mostly growing between patches of cultivation.

Marko said: "Doctor, I'm not sure the wind will take us over the top of that table land. It may take us to the left of the island."

"I am not positive, either," replied the philosopher. "If I knew definitely that we should miss the cliffs, I should set us down in the water and try to swim to the landing place."

He pointed to a tiny stretch of beach, whence a path cut in the cliffside led about halfway up the cliffs. There it ended on a ledge. Directly above the ledge, on the edge of the cliff, Marko saw what looked like a rope ladder rolled up on a reel. He stared down at the water, where choppy waves smashed against the base of the cliff, and said:

"I was the best swimmer in Skudra, but I don't think I could live through that. That water's rougher than it looks from up here."

"We don't realize the force of the wind, because we move with it. If we can alight on the top, fine. If I see we cannot, I will set us down in the water. Perhaps we can work our way around over the talus when the surf subsides."

Marko still looked doubtfully at the surf, since little talus showed above the waves. He said:

"I hope the balloon decides to do one thing or the other. I should hate to pull the rip cord and then miss the edge by a foot."

"Prepare to pull," said Halran, valving air.

Marko grasped the cord. He stared fascinated as the cliff rose towards them and the land opened out. The course of the balloon was tangent to the curve of this edge. A yard to the right, and they would be safe on the mesa; a yard to the left, and they would tumble off into the smother a hundred yards below.

"Pull!" screamed Halran, throwing a leg over the side of the basket.

Marko pulled, then gathered up the slack and pulled again. He heard the ripping sound of the slide of the zip fastener, and the basket dropped suddenly. It struck the ground with a mighty jar. Marko staggered, recovered, and started to climb over the side after Halran, who had leaped to the ground at the instant of alighting.

Before Marko could do so, the underside of the stove smote him on the head as the collapsing bag lowered it on the basket. Then the basket overturned as the wind dragged the bag. Marko had an instantaneous picture of the bag (now limp and flapping), the stove, the ropes, and the basket all bumping along the ground in a tangle of which he was the center. He rolled free into the wet phosphor grass.

"Help me!" shrieked Halran, who had seized a fold of the fabric and was trying to drag it back from the edge of the cliff. So close to the edge had they come down that part of the bag hung over the cliff. A good gust might send the whole apparatus off into the sea.

Marko helped Halran to haul the heavy fabric back, fold by fold, until it was all safely away from the edge. He was assisting the philosopher to drive the anchor and a couple of stakes into the ground when voices made him turn.

He faced a group of women wearing knee-length skirts or kilts. Although he could not be sure in the fading light, most of them looked young. Marko strode towards the group, saying:

"I beg your pardon, ladies, but is this—"

The girls turned and ran shrieking; all but one, who stood her ground. She looked youngest of all, a smallish girl, who said:

"Who are you?" She spoke Anglonian, but in a dialect that Marko found hard to follow.

"My name is Marko, and that is Dr. Boert Halran, the philosopher. Is this Mnaenn?"

"Certainly. What are you doing here?"

"The storm blew us out of our course."

"What do you want?"

"Want? Why, you'll have to ask Dr. Halran, but I suppose we should like quarters for the night, or until the wind blows the right way, and then some help in blowing up our balloon again."

"What did you call that thing?"

"A balloon. Dr. Halran has just invented it."

"Oh. The others thought you demons. You may have trouble convincing the Stringiarch you are not."

"Who are you?" said Marko.

"My name is Sinthi."

"Sinthi what?"

"Just Sinthi. We do not have surnames. Where are you from?"

"We set out from Lann before dawn, a few days ago. We have been to Afka and back."

"Great Einstein! You must have ridden the wings of the wind."

"That," said Halran, joining them, "is precisely what we did, young lady. Now if you could see about obtaining us a meal and a place to sleep, we will not be any more trouble than we can avoid."

"I hope I can," said Sinthi. "The Stringiarch will be furious with you for alighting without permission. I suppose you have been to Niok and Roum and Vien and Bahdaed and all the other great cities."

"Yes," said Halran.

"I wish I could go there."

"Don't they let you leave?" said Marko.

"No. Once a witch, always a witch."

They walked slowly towards the settlement. Marko asked: "What sort of witchcraft do you do?"

"I am training to be a pyromancer. I wanted to compound love philters, but they said I lacked talent."

"And what is this cult of Einstein?"

"Why, this is the center of the worship of Einstein, the god of science," said Sinthi.

Marko said: "Our Syncretic Church of Vizantia recognizes Newton as the god of wisdom: one of the subordinate gods along with Napoleon and Columbus and Tchaikovski. But we have no Einstein in our pantheon."

"Well, here Einstein is not only the head god; he is the only real god, the others being mere demigods or saints. We say, 'There is no god but Einstein, and Devgran is his prophet.'"

"Who is Devgran?"

"David Grant, I think it was originally pronounced, the Ancient One who founded Mnaenn at the time of the Descent."

"And is that the temple?" Marko pointed to the domed structure.

"Certainly," said Sinthi.

"What's in it?"

"That houses the Great Fetish of Einstein."

"I've heard of that," said Marko. "Could we see it?"

"Oh, no! Outsiders aren't allowed to see it ever. We hold a special service for it once a year, at which time it is uncovered."

"What is this fetish?" asked Marko.

"Oh, I don't think I should tell you."

"A statue, is it not?" said Halran innocently. "A golden statue of Einstein holding a mountain in one hand and hurling a thunderbolt with the other—"

"No!" cried Sinthi. "Einstein, being pure spirit, is incorporeal and cannot be depicted."

"Oh, I must have been misinformed," said Halran. "Then the story is true that it is in the form of a geometrical figure, with gems at the angles—"

"Nothing of the sort! The fetish is a pile of boxes about so high." She indicated the height of a yard. "Each box—" She clapped a hand over her mouth. "You mainlanders are too clever for me!"

"Well, well," said Halran in a fatherly way, "now that we know so much, you might as well tell us the rest. It is not as though we intended to harm or desecrate the sacred object."

"Well, each box is made of a transparent substance, like glass but flexible, and inside each box is a stack of cards about the size of your hand. These cards have a spotty look, but there is no writing on them as far as anybody can see. Still, the Prophecy of Anjla says the reign of the Witches of Mnaenn shall end when a man-child of Mnaenn shall read the wisdom of the Ancient Ones from the cards of the Fetish. But that is of course impossible."

"Why?" said Marko.

"Anjla prophesied hundreds of years ago. At once, the Stringiarch adopted the policy of killing all male children at birth, instead of selling them, so that their rule could never be ended."

"So that," said Marko, "is why you witches get your male customers to father your children?"

"Yes. But I've never had one yet. The older witches get the first claim on them. By the time the clients finish with them, they are no longer interested in us younger ones."

Marko clucked disapprovingly. It would be a mighty man indeed who could work his way down through the whole hierarchy.

A trumpet blew in the twilight, and figures appeared running. A lantern with a reflector cast its spotlight on Marko and Halran.

"Surrender!" cried a high female voice in the accents of Mnaenn. "Drop that ax, foreigner, or we'll fill you with bolts!"

Marko saw that, of those who approached, several carried cocked crossbows. At that range they could hardly miss, even in the near-dark. Neither man wore any armor. Even if they successfully bolted now, they could not escape from the island without help in reinflating their balloon.

"They have us," said Halran. "Oh, why did I ever set out on this rash venture. . . ."

Marko drew his ax from its sheath and tossed it on the ground.

"March!" cried the same high voice.

"Madam," said Marko, "we're only harmless travelers who—"

"Silence!"

In the town of Mnaenn, the houses were small but solidly built of the island's black basaltic rock. They were broad and squat in outline, as if the builders feared that hurricanes would blow them away.

More witches appeared in the doorways, looking with frank curiosity at the captives. Marko caught comments on his appearance and suppositious attributes that made him blush.

The houses became larger as they approached the temple in the center. The temple was a big structure, with three stories towering over the rest of the town. From the great central dome, wings rambled off in eight different directions.

The escort herded Marko and Halran into the door at the end of one of these wings and down a long corridor.

By the lamplight of the interior, Marko had a better chance to see his captors. They were all armed women, wearing polished brass cuirasses molded to accommodate the female form, crested brass burgonets on their heads, and kilts. Some carried crossbows and some light pikes. All had blades—one could call them large daggers or small swords—hung from their belts. They did not look very formidable; but Marko reminded himself that, even if he were twice as burly, a jab from a sharp spearhead would let out his life no matter who did it.

The women did not wear the cosmetics affected by those of the Anglonian cities, but they were neater and more attractive than the slatternly hill women of Vizantia. The frequency of light hair and blue eyes bespoke Anglonian or Eropian ancestry. Sinthi had come in with the rest. Marko saw that she had greenish eyes and brown hair with a strong reddish cast. She was a well-rounded, buxom girl, not exactly beautiful, but good-looking in a wind-blown, healthy way.

※※※

Marko was escorted into a room where sat an elderly woman, lean and hard-looking. The female soldiers clanked to attention. The oldest, who had screeched at the travelers, laid Marko's ax on the desk and told her story. Marko could not get all of it because she spoke fast in her strong dialect, but he gathered that he and Halran were suspected of designs on the Great Fetish.

The lean old woman glared at the two men and spoke to Halran: "I am the Stringiarch Katlin. Tell your tale, foreigner."

Halran began: "It is this way, my lady. I am Dr. Boert Halran, philosopher, on leave from the faculty of the University of Lann. I have been engaged in some experiments of unparalleled significance . . ."

Halran wandered off into the technicalities of aerostatics, getting more and more abstruse until Katlin interrupted him: "I suppose you are speaking Anglonian, though it makes no sense to me whatever. I shall merely comment that you philosophers can look for little mercy from us, if by your inventions you learn to duplicate all the thaumaturgies we effect by magic and thus deprive us of our livelihood. All right, Fats, tell your story, and try to keep to the point more closely than this old rattlepate."

Marko said: "My lady, I'm Marko Prokopiu, Dr. Halran's assistant. He invented this balloon, as he tried to tell you. We set out in it to fly to Vien, but the storm blew us out of our course so that we had to light on Afka. When we persuaded the Afkans to let us depart, a calm delayed our return to the mainland, so that we had to put down here. We sincerely apologize for trespassing and will leave as soon as we can reinflate our balloon, assuming the present wind holds."

"A likely story," snapped the Stringiarch. "I shall soon learn if it be true and what to do with you. Put them in a cell and summon the head sibyl."

The female soldiers led Marko and his companion away, down more halls, turning this way and that until Marko was completely confused. They went down a flight of stairs, through a door of bronzen bars, which clanged behind them, and into a cell with a similar door. The guards locked this door, too, and marched away. The captives were left in semidarkness, relieved only by the faint glow of a lantern in a wall bracket down the corridor.

◈◈◈ X ◈◈◈

Nothing happened for so long that Marko thought the next day must be approaching. The mercurial Halran sat with his head in his hands, moaning: "Oh, what a fool I have been, to take such chances at this season! Now we are surely doomed—"

"Hush," growled Marko. "Someone's coming."

There were light, quick steps in the corridor. Somebody

stood at the bars, and Marko saw that it was the young girl who had first greeted them on Mnaenn.

"Sinthi!" said Marko.

"Don't shout!" she said. "You must escape because they have decided to kill you and I will if only . . . and it must be soon because . . . so I'll give you . . ."

"Get your breath, child," said Boert Halran, his despondency gone.

Sinthi gulped air and resumed: "The hierarchy has decided to slay you."

"Why?" said Marko. "What have we done? And don't they try people here as in civilized countries? Even the Afkans decided we were harmless."

"Oh, you have been tried."

"I wasn't aware of it."

"Well, you see, the trials here differ from those of the mainland. They're by divination."

"Oh?"

"Yes. The method of divination is selected at random from the *Handbook of Vaticination,* by thrusting a dagger between the leaves. In your case, the method chosen was by marwan trance. The sibyl went into her trance and saw you two with your necks across the altar rail, and the Stringiarch chopping off your heads with your own ax, to the glory of Einstein."

"Ugh," said Marko.

"I wasn't supposed to know about this, but I listened through the crack of the door. They had an argument. Mera objected that, while they might manage with Dr. Halran, Master Prokopiu was too big to lay his head peaceably on the rail. He might break loose and start chopping them instead. Valri, the suffragan, objected that the Stringiarch wasn't strong enough at her age, especially considering how thick Master Prokopiu's neck is, and she might miss and gash the altar rail. Klaer was against the whole project as barbarous, as there hasn't been a human sacrifice on Mnaenn in nearly a century."

Marko asked: "Why didn't they dismiss the whole idea?"

"No, Katlin insisted. She's very pious, you know. But she admitted she couldn't take off your head with one neat slice. So in the morning they will send the troopers down here to shoot you with crossbows. Then they'll drag your bodies out and lay them on the talisman table in front of the altar and ceremonially cut off your heads, probably with a saw."

"Oh, dear!" said Halran. "That is terrible. Marko, do something! Think of something! Get us out of here!"

Marko said: "Sinthi, did you mention getting us out?"

"I can."

"How?"

Sinthi held up a bunch of keys.

Marko said: "What do we do when we get out?"

"I don't know. I thought you could lower the rope ladder, climb down, and take one of our fishing smacks."

"How big are they?"

"Oh, one or two can row them. But I forgot a squad of guards is stationed at the ladder, as that's where an invader would come up."

Halran said: "I doubt if any such small boat could live through the sea out there anyway. But if I could get help in filling my balloon . . ."

Sinthi said: "What would you need for that?"

"Oh, perhaps a dozen hands and a supply of peat. I could direct them to rig the bag for inflation, and by morning we should be ready to go."

Marko grunted: "I can see the old Stringiarch saying yes, gentlemen, gladly. Unless . . ." He turned to Sinthi. "Where is she now?"

"Asleep, I suppose. Everybody has retired except the witch who has the temple guard. That's how I stole these keys so easily."

"You don't keep a heavy guard around here?"

"Why should we? There is hardly any crime among us; these cells haven't been used for months. We do keep a watch on the cliffs against invaders from outside."

"Where does the Stringiarch sleep?" asked Marko.

"At the end of the second floor of the fourth wing. You go up the stairs, and turn sharply to your left, and down that hall, and up another stairs, and back towards the center . . ."

Marko made Sinthi repeat her complicated directions slowly several times, until he thought that he had them memorized. She had the exasperating female habit of saying "up" or "down" a passage when referring to horizontal movement, and it cost Marko some mental gymnastics to translate her directions into compass points. She said:

"You are not planning to hurt Katlin, I hope? Even though I don't like her, I should not wish to be a party to her murder."

"Not at all," said Marko. "If I can get something with a sharp point, I'll persuade her to order her people to help us off."

He held out his hand for the keys, but Sinthi moved back from the bars, saying: "Oh, no, there's a condition."

"So?"

"You must take me with you."

"Oh?" Marko exchanged looks with Halran, who said: "I fear, my dear, our balloon will not carry that much weight."

"It would raise me and one of you, wouldn't it?"

"Neither of us would leave the other," said Marko.

"No ride, no keys," said Sinthi.

"Oh, come," said Marko. "Why are you so anxious to leave?"

"Because I hate this place. I'm bored to death. I don't want to be a pyromancer and spend my life staring into fires to see visions. I think that is all a lot of nonsense anyway. I want to be a housewife, like the mainland girls, and have a man and a home to myself . . ." A tear glimmered.

Marko thought, then said: "I should be glad to take you, but Dr. Halran knows what he's talking about. There is no point in our all taking off, only to come down in the sea five minutes later. I'll tell you . . ."

"Tell me what?" she said as Marko paused.

"I swear by all the gods that if you help us to get out of here, I will do my best to come back and fetch you too."

"Well . . ."

"Look," said Marko. "I'm a Vizantian. You have heard, haven't you, how punctilious Vizantians are about keeping their word?"

"Y-yes, though I suspect you aren't always so careful as you claim." She hesitated again. "All right, I'll do it. But if you play me false, I'll cast every kind of spell in the arsenal of Mnaenn, from *envoûtement* down."

Marko smiled. "I thought you didn't believe in them?"

"I don't exactly disbelieve in them either. One of them just might work. Here, take your keys, but give me time to get back to my dormitory before you break out. I don't want to be connected with your escape."

"If I count five hundred, will that be enough?"

"I think so, if you don't count too fast. Good-bye and good luck."

§§§

Marko and Halran waited until Marko had counted. Then Marko tried keys until he found one that unlocked the door of their cell. He started out, then turned to the philosopher.

"We can't go clumping through the halls this way," he whispered, indicating his own heavy boots and Halran's low but substantial shoes.

They removed their footgear and issued forth carrying them. Marko, following Sinthi's directions, led his companion up flights of stone steps and around bends and turns in never-ending corridors. There was no sound, and the only light was that of occasional lamps turned down for the night.

They halted at a pair of large closed doors. Halran murmured: "I am sure this is where she said to turn right, which would take us through these doors."

"No, no," said Marko. "She meant to continue north until the corridor itself turned."

They argued in whispers. Finally, Halran said: "Well, let us at least look to discern what is beyond this door."

Marko cautiously tried the handle. The right-hand door opened with a faint squeak, and behind him Halran drew in his breath.

They had blundered into the cella of the temple. The only light was that of a single lamp, on what Marko recognized as the talisman table. Its light did not reach far. From the darkness above, faint reflections winked back from the jewels and precious metals of the decorations.

Marko shut the door behind them and tiptoed to the center of the structure. Behind them ranked the pews; before them stood the table with its lamp. Beyond the talisman table was a big, massive railing. Marko glanced at Halran and made a chopping motion with the edge of his palm. He laid down his boots and climbed over the rail.

Behind the rail rose the altar, a pyramidal structure with a half-dozen steps going up on each side. Another table or similar support rose from its top. Something else stood atop this. The thing on the support and most of the support itself were hidden by a cloth of gold draped over them.

Marko pulled off the cloth and saw the Great Fetish. Just as Sinthi had said, it consisted of a stack of small boxes of transparent substance, each a little bigger than a pack of playing cards. The boxes themselves were arranged in pyramidal fashion. Marko guessed that there were forty or fifty boxes.

Marko said: "Let's take these with us."

"All of them?"

"Why not?"

"For one thing, we cannot afford the weight. For another, if you take them all, the witches will notice the loss and will probably tear us to pieces, even if we hold their high priestess as hostage. If you put a couple in your pockets . . ."

Without further argument, Marko worked the two topmost boxes of the top stack out of the golden string that bound the stack together and stowed them in his sheepskin. The removal of the boxes left the string limp and loose. To make his theft less patent, Marko gathered up a loop of it and tied it. Then he replaced the cloth of gold.

They stole out of the cella and closed the door behind them. Marko whispered:

"I know where I am now. Down that corridor is the office where the Stringiarch interviewed us. Come on."

"Why?"

"You'll see."

Marko hastened down the corridor and into the office. There was no light inside, but enough came through the door so that his eyes, now accustomed to the dimness, made out the furnishings. He hunted for his ax, but it was not on the desk and not suspended from the walls. Finally he began opening desk drawers, which stuck and squeaked until Halran emitted a terrified hiss:

"Curse you, Marko, be quiet! You will have—"

At that instant Marko tried the last drawer, which stuck, then gave with a piercing squeal. His hand, groping in the dark, found the hilt of his ax just as the door opened wider and a female voice cried:

"Ho! What—"

The Great Fetish

A glimpse showed Marko the silhouette of a witch in half armor, with a spear over her shoulder. He plunged around the corner of the desk and at the woman, knocking Halran flat in his rush. Before she could say a third word, he struck.

The Vizantian culture pattern included rough chivalry on the part of the men towards their women, as long as the women adhered to the sexual code. Therefore Marko smote the watch-woman with the flat of his ax, not the blade. The blow crashed down on her brazen helmet and knocked her to the floor, with the clatter of a hundred overturned fire irons.

"Oh, gods!" breathed Halran in the silence that followed. "We are done for!"

Marko dragged the woman's body all the way into the room and softly closed the door. Now they were in total darkness. Marko pressed his ear to the door. He thought he heard a voice call a question; then nothing but silence.

"She is still alive," came Halran's whisper.

"I only tapped her with the flat to stun her. Take her sword."

"But—but I know nothing of weaponry . . ."

"Oh, Earth! Carry my boots then. Here. Had I known I should meet her . . ."

Marko took the little sword himself. "Come along."

After another long stalk and climbing another flight of stairs, they found themselves outside the room of the Stringiarch. Marko tried the door of dwarf-stupa wood. It was locked.

He fumbled at it without effect, then said: "It doesn't

look very strong. I think I could burst it with a good lunge. But if I miss the first time . . ."

"I understand," said Halran. "Would it not be better to chop it open?"

"No, that would take several licks. The noise would bring the witches. Stand back."

Marko sprang across the corridor and hurled his weight against the door. It was held in place by a light bolt on the inside, the bolt plate in its turn being secured by four nails. As Marko's weight struck the door, the bolt plate flew across the room. The door slapped open. Marko staggered across the room before he could stop himself.

The room was a sitting parlor, not a bedroom faintly lit by a turned-down lamp on a table. Marko heard a sharp voice:

"Who is there? What is it?"

Guided by the voice, he plunged into the bedroom, found the bed, and touched the point of his sword-knife to the chest of the Stringiarch just as she sat up.

"Be quiet and do as you're told, and you shall live," he said.

Voices sounded in the corridor. Halran tumbled into the bedroom. "The witches!"

"Tell them to stay out," grated Marko, pressing his point a little harder.

"S-stay out, girls!" said Katlin. "Now, what do you two brigands want?"

"To leave," said Marko. "Doctor, explain to our hostess."

Halran gave directions for starting a peat fire and inflating the balloon. At the mention of the quantity of peat, Katlin balked. "Ridiculous!" she cried. "We have to import every bit of peat, as there is none on the island. You—"

She subsided as Marko pressed a little harder, and said: "How long will this take?" Marko could not help admiring her coolness.

"What time is it now?" said Halran.

"Only about half-past fifteen. I had just gone to sleep."

"It will take at least till dawn," said Halran.

"And," added Marko, "every minute I shall have the point of this against you, and the first false move . . ."

"Spare me your melodramatics, sir brigand," said Katlin, throwing off her covers. "I trust you would not force me to stand naked all night on the cliff edge?"

"No," said Marko, covering his embarrassment by handing his ax to Halran. "Stand in the doorway, Doctor, in case she gets past me. Dress, madam."

Stringiarch Katlin covered her lean shape with clothes, while Marko stood guard. When she had finished, he seized her wrist, bent her left arm behind her, and marched her out with the point of the sword pricking the skin of her back.

※※※

Muphrid was well up in a clear turquoise sky when the balloon was inflated. Boert Halran tested the wind and said:

"Jump in, Marko."

Halran pulled loose the canvas tube that led from the big peat stove, which the witches had woman-handled out to the site of the balloon. He swung aboard. Marko, still gripping the Stringiarch's wrist, tossed his short sword into the basket and climbed in after.

"Cast off those ropes!" commanded Halran.

He emptied a couple of ballast bags. The witches untied the ropes belayed to the stakes that held the balloon down. Marko let go of Katlin's arm as the balloon rushed up and away.

The instant Marko released her, the Stringiarch sprang away from the basket. "Bows!" she screamed. "Arbalests!"

From the nearest clump of dwarf stupas, a group of witches ran with crossbows cocked. When they came to the place from which the balloon had ascended, they raised their weapons.

The balloon was swiftly rising and drifting westward. The travelers were still within crossbow range. Boert Halran leaned over the side of the basket, placed the thumbs of his outspread hands against his ears, wiggled his fingers, stuck out his tongue, and yelled: "Yah, yah, yah!"

The bowstrings snapped. Both men ducked below the edge of the balloon. Two bolts struck the basket. Another glanced from the small peat stove above with a clang, while the rest screamed past. By the time the arbalesters had cocked their weapons again, the balloon was out of effective range. Two of the warrior women tried long shots anyway. The bolts streaked upwards, slowed, hung for an instant, and sank back towards the ground.

Mnaenn sank and dwindled until the people were mere ants. Marko said: "Whatever possessed you to hoot at them in that undignified way, Doctor?"

Halran replied: "Had I not, they might have shot at the bag, which they could easily have hit."

"Would the escape of air through the holes have forced us down?"

"I do not know. I do not think that one or two small punctures would force us down much sooner than we should have to descend anyway. But such a hole might start a rip in the fabric, which would drop us like a stone."

"Oh," said Marko.

"Again I owe you thanks, Marko. I am a peaceful fellow, who has not struck a blow in anger since boyhood. Without your iron nerves and steel muscles, I should now be as dead as the Ancient Ones; and without your quick wit, my head would be an Afkan trophy."

Marko blushed. "Please, Doctor. You know I'm not really proud of the few little things I did, because I had to. What I really want is an earned university degree."

"Now, is that not the contrary human race?" said Halran. "When I was young, I yearned to be a mighty athlete and adventurer. Being a spindly, awkward little tersor, I had no chance. You, with enough might for two men, would rather be a pale, hollow-chested scholar. If the gods made man, which I doubt, they should have made him so he sometimes enjoyed what he has instead of forever yearning for what he has not."

"If they had, we should probably be mere animals," said Marko. "Whither are we bound now?"

Halran unfolded his chart. "At this rate, we should reach the Eropian coast in about six hours. It will not, however, be the part of Eropia to which we wish to go. We should come down somewhere around Ambur or Pari. And now, if you will excuse me, I think I am going to faint."

XI

Marko slept through most of the next leg. They crossed the Eropian coast around noon.

The country over which they drifted was thickly settled. When they passed low over a town or village, Marko would sometimes see groups of Eropians running about and pointing at the balloon.

Marko felt sad because he had not been able to bring

Sinthi along. While of course he hardly knew her, she impressed him as the sort of girl a man like himself needed. He was particularly attracted by her self-confessed virginity. To find an Anglonian girl over sixteen with that status was apparently impossible.

As the afternoon wore on, the ballast and peat ran low. Halran lowered the drag rope so that its lower end trailed on the ground. This acted as an automatic height governor. When the balloon sank, more of the rope lay on the ground; the balloon, relieved of its weight, rose again. By saving them the necessity of constantly valving air and dropping ballast to keep their altitude adjusted, this simple device stretched their flight for many miles.

The ground, however, came nearer and nearer despite the drag rope. Halran said: "Marko, keep an eye open for a good, firm-looking field near a road. And I do not wish to squash anybody's crops if I can avoid it."

As the balloon sank, Marko sighted a suitable field. The field was being plowed by an Eropian peasant with a team of oxen.

Halran valved air until the basket skimmed along a few feet above the ground. The peasant abandoned his team to run madly away. The oxen bellowed and ran, too. When they had crossed a couple of fields, they forgot their fright and fell to eating.

"Pull!" cried Halran.

Marko pulled the rip cord. Down they came. They climbed out of the tangle and set to work to unfasten the ropes and fold up the bag for transportation.

They were hard at this task when voices made Marko turn. A group of Eropians was approaching over the soft earth: stocky men with little round dark-cloth caps on their heads and pitchforks and other implements in their hands.

"Well?" said Marko, facing them.

The Eropians jabbered and gestured. One seemed to be haranguing the others to attack the aeronauts.

Marko had a fair reading knowledge of Eropian but could not understand it when spoken fast in a local dialect. The peasants' hostile intentions, however, were so obvious that he took hold of his ax.

"Wait, Marko," said Halran, and spoke to the Eropians in their own tongue.

The peasants looked at Halran and began arguing among themselves louder than ever.

"They think we are demons," said Halran. "Ugh. They look dangerous. There is nothing so dangerous as an ignorant and frightened man."

He spoke again, shouting to make himself heard. The peasants paid him no heed. Instead, they began working themselves up to a rage. They shook their fists, screamed, spat, and jumped up and down, waving their implements and shouting threats. Marko said:

"Doctor, take that little sword. If they start for us, our best tactic will be to charge them."

"Oh, no, Marko! Do not antagonize them!" cried Halran. "If I can only make them listen to reason . . ."

Marko took out his ax, slipped off his sheepskin jacket, and wound the garment around his left arm for a shield. If he could kill a few, the rest would run.

Before the battle could be joined, however, hoofs beat upon the nearby road. A rider pulled up and walked his mount over to the crowd, shouting an order. The rider wore one of the most gorgeous costumes that Marko had ever seen. It included a tall cylindrical hat with a shiny black peak and a brass ornament on the front, a red coat with brass buttons, and high, shiny black boots. In his hand, the man bore a long saber.

At the arrival of this personage, all the peasants faced about, dropped their hoes and forks, and sank to one knee with their heads bowed. Then they rose up and began pointing at the travelers and jabbering.

The rider rode closer and shouted a string of questions, which Marko took to mean "Who are you? Where do you come from? What are your names? Where were you born? What is your citizenship? What is your occupation? What are you doing here?"

Halran answered. The mounted man snapped: "Is it true that, as these clodhoppers say, you came down from the sky?"

"Yes, sir," began Halran, but the mounted man interrupted:

"You are under arrest for illegal immigration, practicing magic without a license, and disorderly conduct. Show your papers."

Marko had been astonished, when they first set out, at the number and variety of papers his friend had felt obliged to obtain before journeying to Eropia. Halran had assured him that, to visit that country, one could not have too many. Now Halran handed this mass of documents up. The mounted man sheathed his sword, raised a lorgnette to his eyes, and went through the papers. Apparently he read every one through. The peasants stood in a knot in the background, muttering.

At last the mounted man handed back the papers. He folded up his lorgnette, drew his sword, twirled it in some sort of complicated salute, and sheathed it again. This time he spoke in Anglonian, albeit with a strong accent:

"A thousand pardons, Your Excellencies! A million pardons for having inconvenienced you! But, you understand, I am but a humble policeman and as such must do my duty. Patrolman Jakom Szneider, at your service. Sir Doctor, if you will have the inexpressible goodness to follow me to the police station in Utrec, I will arrange for the issuance of internal-travel papers for you."

"What do you mean by that?" said Halran.

"Oh, these papers allow you to enter Eropia, but you need special permits to travel from one province to another. Have no fear. Utrec is only a mile down the road, and I will walk these papers through myself."

"How about arranging transportation to Vien for my balloon?" said Halran.

"That can be done in Utrec. Let me think—Einri Lafonten has a big wagon and a four-horse team. Of course, you as a foreigner must have a special license to employ a native Eropian. You must also swear to do no work in Eropia that would compete with one of our artisans' guilds, and there are also some small taxes. But fear not. I, Jakom Szneider, will expedite matters with incredible dispatch!"

"Where is Utrec, officer?" asked Halran.

"Why, there!" said Szneider, pointing. "You can see the roofs."

"I mean, where is it on the map? What is it near?"

"Oh? We are about fifty miles northwest of Pari."

Halran groaned. "That means several hundred miles from Vien, and the accursed convention opens tomorrow!"

"Why can you not fly your machine to Vien?" asked Szneider.

Halran explained that balloons went with the wind only, and they came to Utrec.

⁂

Three days later, the wagon of Einri Lafonten, bearing Boert Halran, Marko Prokopiu, and the former's balloon, rattled into Vien, an old gray city built on the inside of a bend in the Dunau River.

During this stage of their journey, Marko had come to appreciate Halran's skill as a traveler in civilized countries. In this land, forms and regulations attended every step, the all-powerful government had its fingers in everything, and everybody expected a tip. Patrolman Szneider, for instance, had helped them not out of the goodness of his heart, but because he assumed that Halran would give him a generous present at parting. Back in Vizantia, to proffer money not due and asked for was an insult to the honor of the person to whom it was offered. Travelers had sometimes been struck dead for offering a proud Vizantian a gratuity. Other lands, other customs, Marko kept reminding himself.

The guards at the gates of Vien, as usual, pored over Halran's papers for half an hour before letting the wagon in. Einri Lafonten's driver drove them over the winding cobblestoned streets, past the ornately carven mansions of the magnates whose power Alzander Mirabo had broken. They stopped at the old city hall, which had been turned over to the philosophers for their convention.

The convention hall was guarded by troopers of the Prem's imperial guard, clad in clain mail from head to foot, with cylindrical barbutes on their heads and halberds in their hands. Inside the grounds, Marko could see small groups of men, and a few women, walking about outside the building. The Eropians could be distinguished by their shaven heads. Being bald, the Prem had shaved off what little hair he had. This made the egghead the official fashion.

After more paper shuffling, the guards admitted the wagon to the convention hall's grounds. Several men approached. Halran called greetings to some of them. A big stout fellow, with a red beard all over his chest, came forward through the gathering crowd crying:

"Boert! What in Earth's name are you doing here?"

"Bringing my balloon to the convention, as I said I would," replied Halran.

"You fool, don't you know that once you're in, they won't let you out again?"

&&&

"Come to the parlor where we can talk," said the red-bearded man. Halran introduced him to Marko as Ulf Toskano, a mathematician and the chairman of the convention.

"But what is this all about?" said Halran plaintively. "After all the perils we have surmounted to get here . . ."

Toskano said: "You should have got here at the opening, if you were bound to get caught in the trap anyway. You missed the wonderful demonstrations by the Chimei brothers yesterday."

"Who are the Chimei brothers, sir?" asked Marko.

"Opticists from Mingkwo. They have done the most amazing thing. Ryoske Chimei has invented a thing he calls a telescope, which makes far things look near, while Dama Chimei has invented one he calls a microscope, which makes small things look large. They had the place in an uproar yesterday.

"We stood in a line a hundred yards long to look through the telescope, which shows a score of stars where we can see but one with our bare eyes. It shows the mountains and valleys of the moons. It is too bad the sky is now overcast, but perhaps Dama Chimei will let you see his microscope. The sight of a drop of stagnant water under that thing will give you nightmares. This is the biggest development since the steam engine. But then this morning, the Prem threw his guards around the hall and announced this idiotic debate."

Toskano pushed open a massive stupa-wood door and led them into the vestibule. Through the doors of the main auditorium, Marko glimpsed the backs of an audience listening to arguments among a small group of men seated on a stage.

Marko said: "What's going on in there, sir?"

Toskano explained: "A panel discussion on that same old subject: Can steam power be applied to land transportation? I proved long ago it's impossible. You can build a little brass model that will pull a couple of wagons across a table top, but the minute you try to go into larger sizes, the weight factors defeat you."

Toskano led them up a flight of stairs and into a large room. There were armchairs and tables, on which books and periodicals were piled. Philosophers sat about smoking, reading, talking in low voices, playing vrizh or chess, or just sitting. Halran wailed:

"But what is this fatal debate?"

"Calm down, Boert. If you're going to die, it might as well be like a man. You know there has been a tremendous to-do in Eropia about the Descensionist theory. The archaeologists and historians claim they now have almost conclusive evidence for it, while the Eclectic Church denounces it and demands that the old heresy laws be applied against us.

"The common people are all excited too, some for and some against, although not one in a hundred really knows what it's about. It's got so we dare not wear our academic robes abroad for fear of having stones thrown at us. Maybe the Philosophers' Guild should have bent with the wind, but instead of that we defied the Evolutionists and petitioned Mirabo to disestablish the Church."

"Well?" said Halran.

"This morning the Prem announced that, tomorrow afternoon, there should be a grand debate between the Descensionists and the Evolutionists, to settle the question once and for all. If he decides the Descensionists are right, he will disestablish the church and execute all the priests, whereas if the Evolutionists win he will cut off all *our* heads."

"Good gods!" said Halran and Marko together. Halran added: "Is the man insane?"

"No; that's just the emphatic way our little Prem does things. Whichever side is right—or whichever he thinks is right—can have anything it asks, while the side that is wrong has been misleading the masses and must die as a crowd of dangerous liars and subversive demagogues."

Halran wailed: "Oh, curses! curses! Why was I born? I shall appeal to the Prez of Anglonia! Can we smuggle out a message?"

"Perhaps, but I doubt if you could get any action from your government before all was over. Besides, from what I hear, your Prez thinks a massacre of philosophers would be good riddance. He's the great peasant leader, and to him nothing that doesn't smell of manure is worth *that*." Toskano snapped his fingers.

Halran pulled himself together. "Then obviously we must win this debate. My friend Master Prokopiu might be of some assistance. He has just been chased out of Vizantia as an incorrigible Descensionist."

"So?" said Toskano. "How is this, Master Prokopiu?"

"I should be glad to help," said Marko. "I have a fair command of the Descensionist arguments as a result of my trial."

Toskano said: "I don't think you would do as a speaker, because your Eropian is not good enough. But I shall appoint you to the committee that is to prepare the debating panel tonight, in case you can contribute a useful suggestion. This will be an all-night task, you know."

Marko said: "Sir, I had rather lose a night's sleep than my head."

"Good. Now tell me about your journey hither. What delayed you?"

Halran summarized the story of their landings on Afka and Mnaenn and their escape from those places.

Ulf Toskano said: "Have you those boxes of cards you took from the Great Fetish?"

Marko brought the boxes out of his pockets and handed them to Toskano, who opened the flap on the end of one box and drew out a card. It was made of a smooth, yellow-white substance. It had the appearance of an ordinary playing card but the feel of being much stronger, as if it were made of metal. On both sides, it was covered with little gray spots arranged in a rectangular pattern, with yellow-white lines between the rows. Toskano handed it back.

"I can make no sense of this," he said. "Let's walk around and look at the exhibits before supper. We shall have enough to do afterwards. It's too bad. Moogan, one of our most effective speakers, was going to deliver a paper on heredity tonight but has begged off because he is too upset about his impending doom."

Toskano led them out of the parlor and down a hall. A series of small chambers had been fitted up as exhibition rooms. One, for instance, contained diagrams showing the theory of one school of naturalists about the proper classification of Kforrian life-forms, with preserved samples of small plants and animals to illustrate.

The next room contained a table on which stood Dama Chimei's microscope, with an assortment of small objects —leaves, fragments of animal tissue, paper, cloth, and so forth—to be seen through it. The Chimei brothers stood at the table answering questions about their device and showing visitors how to operate it. Ryoske Chimei explained, for it seemed that Dama Chimei spoke neither Eropian nor Anglonian. Like other Mingkworen, the Chimei brothers were short men with yellowish skins, straight black hair, and flat faces with wide cheekbones.

"Ha, Dr. Chimei!" said Toskano. "Here are some new visitors to see your marvels. This is Dr. Halran, who has solved the secret of flight, and his assistant Master Prokopiu."

Ryoske Chimei bowed stiffly. "We are honored that persons of such importance trouble themselves to view our poor trifles," he said in a singsong voice. "If you will wait until this gentleman has finished . . ."

Ryoske Chimei spoke to his brother in Mingkwohwa. Toskano murmured to his companions:

"Don't let that pretense of humility fool you. That's just Mingkwoan manners. They are the most self-conceited fellows I ever met; everything outside of Mingkwo, to them, is barbarous squalor."

"If you please, sirs," said Ryoske Chimei, and Halran bent over the microscope, ohing and ahing as he witnessed the wonders of the microcosmos. While Halran was looking, Ulf Toskano said:

"Master Prokopiu, get out those boxes of cards you brought from Mnaenn. Thank you." He took out a card and handed it to Ryoske Chimei, saying: "Try this under your magnifier."

Ryoske handed the card to Dama Chimei, who slid it under the objective of the microscope.

"Hey!" cried Boert Halran. "Those little gray discolorations are writing!"

"What?" said Toskano. "Don't be ridiculous! Who could write so small that not even the letters could be seen?"

"This is printing."

"But how could it be? For printing, somebody has to cut a type mold; somebody else has to cast a type slug; somebody else has to set the slug in the press—"

"Look yourself." Halran made room for Toskano.

"By Napoleon, it is at that," said the chairman. "But in no language I know. I thought I had a smattering of all the tongues of Kforri."

Halran said: "Many of the letters are like those of our alphabet, but the combinations are strange."

"We need a linguist." Toskano glared about and crossed glances with one of the other philosophers waiting his turn at the microscope. "Bismaak! Do you know Duerer?"

"Yes," said Bismaak.

"Well, try to find him as quickly as you can."

"May I look now?" said Marko.

"As you brought the cards here, I suppose you have a right to," said Toskano.

Under the lens, Marko saw a whole page of type set in double columns. This page, he found by moving the card slightly, was one of the little gray spots, no larger than the head of a large pin. Under the glass, it was enlarged until it was just legible.

Bismaak returned with a whiskered man introduced as Duerer, who took one look into the microscope and cried:

"This is Old Anglonian! I can read a little of it, but we need Domingo Bivar. He has devoted his life to the study of the few writings and inscriptions we have in that language. I'll fetch him."

Duerer departed at a run. After some wait, he returned in his turn with a small man, dark like an Arabistani. The newcomer, introduced as Domingo Bivar, was identified as an Iverianan by the length of his hair, which hung almost to his shoulders. Dr. Bivar looked into the microscope and began to hop up and down as if the floor had become hot.

"This is a thing most extraordinary!" he shrilled. "Let me see another of the cards, for favor."

After further scrutiny he said: "Dr. Toskano, I must have the microscope, much notepaper, much coffee, and the undisturbed use of the room till tomorrow. May I?"

After much palaver, it was agreed that Bivar should have unrestricted use of the microscope until the following day. The Chimei brothers made it understood that they would stay in the room to supervise.

※ ※ ※

At supper, Marko saw the entire membership of the convention. Aside from the fact that some wore the garb of distant lands, like Arabistan and Mingkwo, there was nothing special about the philosophers. They looked just like people, to Marko's faint disappointment. But he consoled himself with the thought that if this were the case, nobody would object to recognizing him as a philosopher on the ground of appearance.

The committee for preparing the debate met after supper. Marko sat in with the rest. He soon found that his own knowledge of the Descensionist controversy was too elementary to be of much help here. When he made a suggestion, they turned on him saying:

"Yes, my dear Master Prokopiu, but if you had been here this afternoon you would know that we went over that idea first of all."

So Marko was reduced to sitting in abashed silence while the experts tossed ideas around. They were hard at it when a knock interrupted them. In came Ulf Toskano with a bearded man in workman's garb. The philosophers stared at the newcomers. One of the former rose and said:

"Greetings, Patriarch Yungbor. What brings Your Excellency into the lair of the enemy?"

There was a scraping of chairs as the others, too, recognized the head of the Holy Eclectic Church. Although some of the philosophers, to judge by their comments, were violently anti-clerical, all had been conditioned to this courtesy.

The Reverend Pier Yungbor sat down heavily at the end of the table. Ardur Mensenrat, the chairman of the committee, said: "How on Kforri did you get here? I thought all you people were under lock and key too."

The patriarch said: "Where the flock is faithful, the shepherd can look for unexpected succor. I take it you gentlemen are planning your side of tomorrow's debate?"

"Right," said Mensenrat.

"I am here to make an unprecedented request. Before I make it, let me say that I have what seem to me excellent reasons. You are philosophers; you pride yourselves on keeping your minds open. Try to keep them open in this case until you have heard me out. It will be difficult."

He stared around the table. Mensenrat said: "Proceed, esteemed sir."

"I ask that you 'throw the game'; that you deliberately lose to us."

The silence became loud. Yungbor looked mildly around the long ellipse and continued:

"You naturally ask why. Well, there are two reasons. The first is practical. Alzander Mirabo, as we all know, has long been hatching war against Iveriana. Specifically, he plans to march over the Equatorial Mountains and take them through their back country. We know the present government of Iveriana, weak and distracted by revolts, could never halt this invasion.

"The Kacike is a foolish old man, who has been preserved from assassination by ambitious subordinates only by their inability to agree upon a successor. His province of Sturia has been in open revolt for years. He sends armies against the Sturians, and his soldiers sell their arms to their enemies and desert. You see how much chance the Iverianans would have against the strongest, best-disciplined army in the world."

A philosopher spoke: "Under those conditions, wouldn't Eropian rule be all to the good?"

"No. For one thing, the Iverianans, however they betray and murder one another, hate foreigners even more and will fight to the last against them. I have been to Iveriana and know. They would practice hit-run, guerrilla war. The Prem would burn cities and slaughter hostages in retaliation, and so on until most Iverianans were dead, together with many of our own people.

"The Eclectic Church has been exerting all its influence against this crime. So far, by playing on the Prem's beliefs, by dangling the hope of Earth and the fear of Space before him, we have held him off. But if he decides we are mistaken, what will hold him back then?

"Another thing. By coöperating with the Syncretic Church in Vizantia and the Latitudinal Church in Anglonia and Barmadislam in Arabistan and so forth, we have prevented any serious outbreak of war for four decades. Would you wish to break this peace?"

Another philosopher spoke up: "Patriarch, we have our ideals too, though you may not believe it."

"I have said no such thing," said Yungbor.

"Specifically, we attach a value to the discovery of truth. We think it's good in itself. In this case we think we have found a particular truth that goes under the name of Descensionism. Would you have us suppress it?"

Yungbor replied: "No doubt you are taking for granted the validity of Czipollon's axiom, 'The true is the right and the right is the true.' Now think, gentlemen. Is there any reason for accepting such an idea as true in the first instance than any other? Take Evolution, for example. Let us suppose—I concede nothing, but merely suppose for the sake of argument—that Descensionism is true. Yet by pressing your belief, by urging it upon the people and their rulers, you may break the peace and touch off a round of wars worse than any seen hitherto on this distracted planet. Be assured, the Anglonians and Vizantians and Mingkworen will not sit idly by while Mirabo aggrandizes himself at the Iverianans' expense. They fear him enough now. And with this flying machine the Anglonians have invented, war will be more terrible than ever.

"In fact, with all these scientific advances of which you so proudly boast, you may one day be able to wipe mankind off Kforri, as the forebears of the present gods are once said in the myths to have done to one another on Earth. Then all we shall need is one lunatic in command of a nation. . . . Well, what is the good in such a case?"

Mensenrat said: "There is one other item, which you have not considered. Our necks."

Yungbor wagged his beard. "That goes without saying. There are ours too. I did not bring this matter up because it is obvious what our respective preferences would be on the level of such sordid motives. I did hope that I could appeal to worthier sentiments.

"And consider this possibility, the second reason whereof I spoke. I know that many of you gentlemen do not accept our creed. You say that this is or is not objectively true, and point to cases where our finite minds have been shown to be mistaken in the past. But consider! This creed, objectively true or not, is logically valid. It has been assembled by our great theologians over half a thousand years. And by means of it we keep the people in order. We restrain their natural violence and swinish lusts. We make it possible for them to live together as civilized men.

"You think you have created civilization with your inventions and discoveries. And, in fact, people got along well enough up to fifty or seventy-five years ago, when your inventions and discoveries began to come so fast that they have revolutionized everybody's thinking. The Church is the only stable institution they have left to cling to. But what good would inventions and discoveries be without a moral force to make people moderate their actions towards each other? How long would they be civilized if, every chance a man had, he knocked his neighbor over the head, dragged him into his kitchen, and cooked and ate him?

"You scoff. You say, *I* should never consider such an act. I lead a moral upright life without supernatural sanctions. But are you gentlemen average citizens? You know the answer to that one. Still less are you members of that large fringe who really prefer evil to good, who revel in wickedness. If you do not believe such people exist, come with me to night court—that is, if we all survive our present peril. So if you convince the Prem of your 'truth' and overthrow our creed, who shall guide the people? Do you think you can do so by equations and formulas, which they cannot even understand?

"Think about what I have said, gentlemen, and thank you for your courtesy in listening to me. Good night."

When the patriarch had gone, there was a moment of silence. A committeeman said: "I may not agree with him, but he's a plausible old devil."

"He is perfectly honest in his way," said another.

"Oh, nonsense!" said another. "All supernaturalism is simply a scheme to enable a class of magicians called priests to live without working."

"Oh, that's not fair at all. . . ."

They argued inconclusively, shying away from the actual decision. It transpired that all of them wanted to save their heads and therefore to win the debate, but they wanted to find a reason for so doing that would not make them look like mere frightened self-seekers. Ardur Mensenrat put it acceptibly:

"In the first place, we don't really know whether our action would be the critical factor in deciding the Prem for war or peace. We have only Yungbor's word for that. If I know Alzander Mirabo, he will have made up his mind long since. If we don't furnish him with a pretext, somebody will.

"In the second, while we should deplore the massacre of the priesthood, if worse come to worst we think we are more important to civilization than they, and that they can be replaced more easily than we.

"Finally, if it were a question of eliminating war forever from Kforri, we might do otherwise. But it is not. Yungbor takes credit for the peace of recent decades, but the historiographers tell a different story. They say it is the result of the balance of power among the major nations. All are armed and touchy, all are full of tribal parochialism, truculent nationalism, and rancorous xenophobia. If the Prem does not go to war now, we have no assurance that somebody else will not do so next month."

There was a common sigh of relief that Mensenrat had put so succinctly the thoughts that others, including Marko Prokopiu, were groping for. Marko's mind had wandered during the debate, which tended to ramble and stray. In phantasy he saw himself gripping the wrist of the Stringiarch and poking the knife into her back, a couple of inches to the left of the spine where it would have a good chance of reaching the heart. . . .

He hesitated, fought down the horrible fear of making a fool of himself, and rapped on the table.

"Yes, Master Prokopiu?" said Mensenrat.

"If you gentlemen will excuse me," said Marko, feeling himself blush, "although I'm but an ignorant backwoods schoolteacher, without even a legitimate degree, I have a suggestion to make."

"Go ahead."

"What I suggest does not conflict with the plans for the debate but might make the debate unnecessary."

"Get to the point, sir," said Mensenrat.

"Well, I was thinking—that is, if we could get control of the person of the Prem, we might hold him as hostage to make him let us go."

"Preposterous!" said somebody.

"Maybe, but what have we to lose? And speaking as one who has just escaped from the Isle of Mnaenn by that means, I think I may claim some small expertise in the science of kidnaping, which has perhaps been denied you learned gentlemen."

"What's your plan?" said Mensenrat.

"Well, the idea has only just dawned upon me, so I shall more or less have to make it up as I go. But, briefly . . ."

XII

The following morning, the eleventh of Perikles, Muphrid rose behind a thin cover of clouds. Marko Prokopiu stood with Boert Halran, Ulf Toskano, and other philosophers watching the inflation of the bag in the courtyard. This time, the balloon was not loaded with much fuel or ballast, because it was meant to be used as a captive balloon only.

Marko's throat hurt from talking most of the night. The philosophers would have argued forever, or until the Prem's executioner came for them, if Mensenrat had not taken Marko's side and bullied the rest into acquiescence. At that, many seemed convinced that if only they did nothing, the danger would go away of its own accord.

An imperial soldier rode up to the guarded gate in front of the building, dismounted, and came in. He clanked up to Toskano, drew his sword, banged his spurs together, saluted, sheathed his sword, and drew a folded paper from the cuff of his gauntlet.

"His ineffable Serenity, the Prem of Eropia, sends you greetings," said the soldier, "and begs that you will have the inexpressible goodness to read this note and return your answer forthwith."

Toskano read the note and said to the philosophers around him: "He's coming. Second hour. Will you be ready, Boert?"

"Easily," said Halran.

Toskano spoke to the soldier: "Have the generous kindness, esteemed sir, to inform your master, the mighty Prem of Eropia, that we shall be overcome with gratitude at his serenity's gracious condescension in visiting our convention and witnessing some of our trivial experiments. All will be ready."

"I cordially thank Your Excellency," said the soldier, and clanked off.

Marko turned back to the balloon, but then came another interruption. Domingo Bivar rushed out of the hall with his long hair flying, waving a fistful of paper. He had bags under his bloodshot eyes.

"Dr. Toskano!" he shouted. "Dr. Toskano! Come quick! All is solved! We win! I must tell you. . . . It is a thing most amazing. . . ."

Toskano asked Halran: "How soon will your balloon be inflated?"

"Not for another hour," said Halran.

Toskano followed Bivar; Marko and a few others followed Toskano. Bivar led them back to the room containing the Chimei microscope. One of the brothers (Marko could not be sure which) was still on guard. The cards were stacked on the table.

Bivar sat down, dropped his notes on the floor, picked them up, reshuffled them, and began: "Gentlemen: what we have here is a record, made by some process long since lost, of the literature of the men of Earth before the Descent."

He waited until the buzz occasioned by this announcement had subsided, then went on: "These little gray spots on the cards are pictures, made by some process chemical, of pages printed. If Dr. Chimei can with a few bits of glass make the small appear large, why cannot the large be made small? But to continue. One of the boxes contained an encyclopedia complete. The other contained a collection of biographies of men of Earth. There were thousands of lives of Earthmen, some as long as whole books in themselves. Why only these two collections should have been preserved, or why the Ancient Ones should have recorded their knowledge in that form—"

Marko said: "Excuse me, Dr. Bivar, but those are not all."

"Not all? You mean there are more?"

"Yes. There were forty or fifty boxes on Mnaenn, but I brought away only those two."

"What? You idiot! Fool! ¡Tonto! ¡Loco! Saphead! Ass! Are you mad, that you did not fetch the rest? You should be—"

Toskano broke into the harangue, and Marko explained why he had not brought more of the boxes.

"Oh," said Bivar. "Pardon, pardon. I did not know. I am overturned, shaken up, and I have not slept since yesterday. Exculpate me, pray! I need that you forgive, sir. But if we escape from the Prem, our greatest duty is to recover the cards remaining, by whatever means necessary.

"To continue. I could not read all these records in one night, naturally, especially as they are in a dead language and are very difficult. Old Anglonian, or English as those who spoke it called it, had a system of spelling very peculiar, in which almost any letter could mean any sound and conversely. There are many words that I do not know, though some I could guess from context.

"To go through all this material is the task of years. All I could do was to skim and skip about. Nor do the records deal with the actual Descent, as they were compiled before that event. They do tell us that Evolution is a correct hypothesis—but on Earth, not on Kforri as far as we are concerned.

"Earth is a planet material, circling a small star near the star Mira. It is a little smaller than Kforri, but more of its surface is covered by water. It is also a little warmer on the average, but the climate is much more extreme, hotter than we are at the equator and colder at the poles. 'Kforri,' I learn, is a corruption of the name for this planet in Old Anglonian: 'K-40.' Earth has a variety of animals, both tame and wild, and five of its six continents are inhabited by men of several different races, differing among themselves much as we do.

"At the time when these records were reproduced in this form, the men of Earth had attained travel from their planet through empty space to other planets of their system or even to planets of other stars."

"How did they fly through space, where there is no air to breathe?" asked Toskano.

"They went in a vehicle tubular that squirts itself through space by blowing a great flame out its rear, and the ship of space is sealed and carries its own air."

Toskano persisted: "How can that work when there's nothing for the flame to push against?"

"I do not know, but let me get on. The other planets of their own system are either too hot or too cold, or do not have the right sort of air, to be comfortable places of dwelling. So they have gone to other stars to settle on their planets. I gather that one of these interstellar trips is a business formidable. It takes years and costs a lot tremendous, so they plan them with the utmost care.

"They send a small ship of space out first, which does not even land on the planet but circles around it, determines its temperature and kind of air, and so forth. Then they send a main expedition of two or three large ships of space with Earthly plants and animals so that they can set up a settlement permanent. Then one of the two or three ships of space will take all the peat, or whatever fuel they use, and fly back to Earth. If all goes well, they may send more ships of space, as they are much crowded for room on Earth.

"Something of the sort must have been done in our case. But for some reason the records were lost, or at least they were taken to Mnaenn and everybody else forgot about them. There must have been some sort of device to read these records, which was lost or broken. Perhaps there was a quarrel among the settlers. I infer that these settlers came from all over the Earth, and in settling here they broke into several groups or tribes, speaking languages different. From these tribes are descended the major nations of today.

"There is much more in here; I have taken notes as you see. The names of our countries and cities are mostly the names of places on Earth, more or less corrupted. Lann is London, Vien is Vienna, Niok is New York, and Mnaenn is named for the Terran isle of Manhattan, which seems to have been another name for New York. The very gods proclaimed by the churches are famous men of Earth. The animals native of Kforri are named after similar animals that live, or have lived, on Earth. Thus 'tersor' and 'transor' are derived from 'pterosaurus' and 'tyrannosaurus,' two extinct Earthly beasts. The jumping lizard that we call a 'rabbit' is named for a hopping animal of similar size and habits on Earth, although the animal terrestrial is a mammal with warm blood like us. The—"

A philosopher put his head in the door and said: "Dr. Toskano, the Prem is arriving."

Toskano jumped up and rushed out, Marko after him.

The Great Fetish

Alzander Mirabo, Prem of Eropia, was just getting down from his huge, paxor-drawn, gilded coach when Marko reached the site of the inflation. The balloon was now almost fully inflated, swaying against the sky. The courtyard was full of kneeling philosophers. Toskano and Marko knelt, too, until they heard the Prem's vibrant voice: "Rise, gentlemen!"

Alzander Mirabo was a small man with a pale, nondescript face, unremarkable save for a certain sharpness of nose, hollowness of cheeks, and pouchiness under the eyes. He wore a plain black uniform with a blued-steel cuirass and helmet, contrasting with the gorgeousness of his aides. He came forward smartly, his heels clicking on the cobblestones, until he reached the balloon.

"Dr. Toskano?" said the tyrant. He recognized the chairman of the convention and stepped forward to give him a brisk handshake. "This is magnificent, Doctor. Where is the inventor? Dr. Halran? I congratulate you. I can already see military applications of this device. It must obviously be socialized. In fact, I consider it so important to the welfare of the masses that I shall order that, even though the philosophers lose this afternoon's debate, you shall be spared. Be so good as to explain how the device works, if you please."

Halran did, stumbling for words. The Prem asked a few questions which surprised Marko by their cogency.

"Are we ready for this flight?" said Mirabo. "I played truant from the work of the Empire for an hour, but already I can see the papers piling up on my desk."

"All ready, sir," said Halran. "You shall ascend with my assistant, Master Marko Prokopiu."

Marko's hand was wrung too. The little man had a steely grip.

"And one of my bodyguards, of course," said Mirabo, indicating a stalwart in chain mail close behind him.

"Oh, but Your Serenity!" said Halran. "I am not certain the balloon will hoist so much weight."

"Well, I'm smaller than average, so that should not much matter. We shall all climb in, at any rate, and if it won't rise, it won't rise."

Halran shot an apprehensive look at Marko, who gave a tiny nod. He thought that he could take care of the bodyguard. The Prem briskly climbed into the basket. The bodyguard followed, and Marko followed the bodyguard.

"Cast off!" said Marko.

The appendix was pulled free, the ropes were slacked off, and the balloon rose. Below, a crew of the burliest philosophers clung to the drag rope.

Up they went, swaying gently and rotating a little. The Prem exclaimed with delight as they ascended above the roofs, and Vien appeared spread out beneath them. Marko saw the loop of the Dunau River on three sides.

"What a view!" cried Mirabo, smiting his fist against his armored chest. "I soar like a tersor! Magnificent!" When they reached the greatest height allowed by the drag rope, the Prem exclaimed: "What a substitute for light cavalry! Now I shall need no more Arabi mercenaries for scouting. Praise be to Napoin! Master Prokopiu, turn around!"

Marko found that the Prem had produced a medal

from his trousers pocket. Mirabo pinned this medal to Marko's chest. "You have merited well of me, Marko. Let this be a small token."

"I earnestly thank Your Serenity," said Marko. "Now just a minute . . ."

His heart pounding with excitement, he stopped, grasped the ankle of the bodyguard, and straightened up, hurling the guard over the edge of the basket.

"Hey!" shouted the Prem, reaching for his sword.

The guard's shriek came up with diminishing amplitude as the man fell. There was a loud slam as the armored body struck the cobblestones two hundred feet below.

Marko snatched up his ax from the floor just as the Prem whipped out his sword and thrust. Marko struck the darting blade aside with the head of his ax and, before Mirabo could execute a remise, whacked him over the helmet with the flat of the ax.

The Prem slumped down in the basket. Marko snatched the sword out of his limp hand, leaned over the side, and threw the weapon away.

The bodyguard lay in a widening pool of blood. The rest of the Prem's entourage were closing in on the philosophers with bared weapons, but Toskano shouted:

"If you kill us, the balloon will fly away!"

The guards hesitated. Marko called down at the faces that looked up at him like a swarm of pink dots:

"Do as I say or I'll throw the Prem over too!"

"What?" shouted an officer.

Marko repeated in full bellow.

"Do what?" said the officer.

"Just a minute," roared Marko. He turned and examined the Prem. The man was still alive, for which Marko was thankful. He had feared that, not knowing his own strength, he might have slain him.

Marko unbuckled the cuirass and the helmet, baring the Prem's nude scalp, and dropped them over, too, tossing them so that they landed on bare cobbles. With a length of rope, he bound the Prem's wrists and ankles. Alzander Mirabo began to come to during this process and had to be quieted by a punch in the jaw.

Marko leaned over again and shouted: "Your Prem is safe while you obey our orders. Dr. Toskano will tell you what to do."

After that, Marko had only to sit in the basket and smoke his pipe while he watched the proceedings. Sometimes he climbed up to stuff a briquette of peat into the auxiliary stove.

Under Toskano's directions, the balloon was towed outside the gate and the drag rope was belayed to the harness of the Prem's paxor. This process caused the paxor to fidget and bellow. Once the rope was fastened, however, the beast, no longer able to see the balloon, forgot about it.

Officers were sent out to round up other vehicles. Those philosophers who lived in Vien scurried away to gather up their families and possessions.

Marko heard the Prem move and looked around to see him sitting on the floor of the basket, glaring up at Marko with bared teeth. His face held all the concentrated malevolence that one human face can. The instant his eye caught Marko's, the scowl was wiped away by a cheerful smile.

"Well, my good man," said Alzander Mirabo, "perhaps you can tell me what this is all about?"

"We philosophers, Your Serenity, were forced by your threat to take this drastic method of getting out of Eropia."

"Oh, you mean that silly debate? You took it seriously?" The Prem gave a little laugh. "My dear fellow, I was only fooling. I should not have cut off anybody's head, no matter who lost. That was just my little joke, to make sure that both sides extended themselves."

Marko rubbed a hand against his bull neck. "Maybe so, sir, but such a joke somehow doesn't seem funny to the owner of the head."

"Now that you mention it, I see your viewpoint. Where is my guard?"

Marko pointed downward.

"I remember now. Dead, I suppose?"

"He looks it."

"Poor Sezar! A brave, faithful, and honest fellow. Aren't you sorry you murdered him?"

Marko had not thought about the guard as a human being, but he said: "I suppose I am, but that's war."

"Well, let's call off this whole fantastic escapade, what do you say? Lower me, and as soon as I'm safely on the ground I will order that all the philosophers be allowed to go free."

Marko looked stonily at his captive.

"There shall be no reprisals, either."

Marko kept silence.

"You don't believe me? Well, I probably shouldn't in your shoes. But see here, this can't go on. You cannot possibly get away with it. You can't seize the person of the head of the world's greatest nation, the commander of the strongest army, like an Arabi kidnaping a caravaner. Put me down! I, the leader of the masses of Eropia, command you! You cannot resist!"

Marko said nothing. Mirabo tried another tack: "Well, while I cannot say I am pleased by this treatment, I can't help admiring the audacity and adroitness with which you carried it out. You ought to have gone to work for me. I still might have a place for you. Why join these mumbling, peering old pedants? Anyone can see you are more the physical type. Why not throw in with me? I can always use a man with your strength and dash."

Marko scowled. The Prem could not know that Marko perversely took no pride in his bulging muscles but was, instead, consumed by the ambition to become a respected scholar. He replied only a curt "No."

For an hour the Prem kept on trying to persuade Marko to let him down. He tried every approach. He threatened, blustered, bribed, wheedled, and appealed to Marko's better nature. He even tried to put Marko to sleep by hypnotism. Nothing worked.

Then the bizarre procession got under way, heading for the south gate. First came the Prem's state coach, an ornate vehicle of glass and gilt as big as a six-horse tally-ho. To the back of the Prem's draft paxor was attached the drag rope that held Halran's balloon, swaying and rotating, while the huge coach rumbled behind. Then came a long line of carriages and wagons crowded with philosophers and their gear and dependents.

"You Vizantian savages are a stubborn lot," said

Mirabo with a sigh, after his victim had shrugged off the tenth effort to get the better of him. "Where are we going?"

"To Massey, sir."

"And then whither?"

"Oh, we thought we might borrow one of your ships."

"I must say, I never thought philosophers could be men of action as well. I'll be more careful whom I play jokes on in the future."

"Oh, I'm nobody at all, sir," said Marko. "I've merely been lucky."

They passed out through the south gate. This took a lot of arranging, because the city wall was continuous above the gate. The drag rope therefore had to be untied, carried over the gate, and reattached on the far side. The circuslike procession rumbled over the bridge across the Dunau and plodded out along the road for Massey, the main seaport of Eropia.

When Marko's supply of peat got low, he replenished it by lowering a small basket by a light rope from the balloon to the ground. When he and his captive got hungry, he hoisted up a meal by the same means.

"You fellows seem to have thought of everything," said the Prem.

"That, sir, is what brains are for."

"Don't I get any coffee?"

"I'm sorry, but I need it all. It won't hurt you to go to sleep, but if I do I might wake up on my way to the ground."

Alzander Mirabo laughed. "You are twice my size! I

couldn't toss you around that way without awakening you."

"You might stab me or something."

"Not if I'm trussed up like this."

"Oh, you might wriggle over and rub your bonds against my ax, like that character in the novel by Shaixper."

The Prem laughed. "Are you a mind reader too?"

Marko grinned. He had merely put himself in the Prem's place. Thus he had kept himself from weakening when the Prem had tried to beguile him with smiles and tempt him with promises. He knew the Prem's reputation for coldblooded perfidy.

XIII

Muphrid had set, but the twilight lingered, when the odd caravan arrived at Massey. Marko watched sleepily as the paxor lumbered down to the docks of the Imperial Navy. There was a long palaver among Toskano, the officer who had come with the procession from Vien, and another officer of the fleet. The philosophers hauled the balloon down to a height of fifty feet. A reflector lantern, shone on the face of the Prem, convinced the naval officers that their lord really was captive.

After another hour's delay, the philosophers detached the balloon from the weary paxor and carried their end of the rope aboard a ship, the steam ram *Incredible*. Marko, who had never been aboard a steamship, watched with interest. The ship was a sturdy-looking craft about two hundred feet long, with a big iron spike at the waterline at her bow, a strip of bronze armor running around her waterline, and a tall, thin funnel in the waist.

The philosophers had planned in advance to insist upon the merest skeleton crew on their ship; just enough to operate the machinery and steer. ("After all," said Voutaer of Roum, "I designed that cursed engine for the Prem, and I ought to know how to run it.")

Prem Mirabo, watching the preparations, asked Marko Prokopiu: "Now that you are ready to set forth, when will you release me?"

"When we reach our destination, sir," said Marko.

"What? But that's impossible! Who knows what conspirators might not seize my desk in my absence?"

Marko shrugged. "I think, sir, we could bear that disaster with becoming fortitude. And didn't you tell me you were the idol of the masses? Surely they'd stand by you!"

"That is no joking matter," grumbled the Prem.

The stack of the *Incredible* began to spit smoke and sparks. The breeze carried the smoke aft until it enveloped the basket and made Marko and the Prem cough and rub their eyes.

"Will you suffocate as well as kidnap me?" groaned Mirabo.

Marko suffered along with his captive through another half hour, until the *Incredible* cast off and put out of the harbor with a great blowing of whistles and bonging of bells. The stack went puff-puff-puff, making Marko and Mirabo cough more than ever. As the lights of the dark quiet harbor slid away behind them, the philosophers hauled the balloon down to the deck.

Marko climbed out, stretching and yawning, and gave a hand to the Prem. The philosophers ringed the stern in helmets and hauberks.

"Your arms locker was well stocked, Your Highness," said Ulf Toskano. "Don't think to set the crew on us, because we outnumber them three to one and have removed all arms out of their reach. We shall also guard you day and night against any untoward event."

Marko mumbled: "Dr. Toskano, where can I sleep?"

※※※

On the fourteenth of Perikles, the *Incredible* raised the Isle of Mnaenn but hung off on the horizon until sunset, so as to make her approach under cover of darkness.

When he had awakened after sleeping most of the night through, Marko had been fascinated by the ship. He spent hours below, watching the great bronze connecting rods heave and the cranks go around. He pestered Voutaer for information on the workings of a steam engine.

The wind rose, and a choppy sea made the *Incredible* pitch like a cork. When she buried her ram, her screw came out and she shook herself like a wet dog. Gusts of rain beat across the slippery deck, and Marko suffered the tortures of seasickness. The Eropian sailors prayed to the sea god Nelson to save them from the terrors of the sea and the spells of the witches of Mnaenn. Some philosophers, who had opposed the conquest of Mnaenn, went about saying "I told you so."

Halran, looking towards Mnaenn, with rainwater dripping from his chin, said: "I do not know how we shall ever get the balloon inflated from this tossing deck." He glanced back gloomily to where the bag thrashed and lunged in its tackle. "I am sure the fabric will rip from this rough handling. If you come down in the sea, Marko, you cannot swim in armor. The mere thought of what you plan gives me the horrors."

Marko answered: "Anything to get off this accursed deck and get my stomach back again. I think I left it fifty miles astern. It's worse than camel back."

"Stop glooming," roared Ulf Toskano, slapping Halran on the back with irritating heartiness. "We ran a bigger risk when we seized the Prem. And this rain will have driven the witches indoors. You might accomplish your task without meeting one."

"I don't count upon that," said Marko. He stood in a suit of three-quarters armor, which had been pieced together out of the largest pieces in the arms locker.

The wind moderated, although the rain continued, as they chuffed towards the island. Before midnight, the *Incredible* stood off the northwest corner of Mnaenn. She presented her stern to the island, with her engine barely turning over and a trysail out to hold her head into the wind. Marko Prokopiu climbed clanking into the basket.

"Cast off," he said.

Away went ropes and ballast. The balloon, swaying and jerking, rose from the stern. Marko heard the fabric strain against its ropes. The philosophers had not lit the auxiliary peat stove, since the balloon would not be aloft long.

The basket swayed like a pendulum. Straining his eyes into the featureless dark, Marko felt a return of his seasickness. The reel paying out the drag rope on the quarterdeck squealed. The jerking eased as more rope was paid out, allowing slack to accumulate between jerks.

Marko stared towards the cliff. In this murk, he could not even tell direction. The balloon had started to rotate, first in one direction and then in the other.

There was nothing to do but grip the edge of the basket, feel his ax for the hundredth time, and try to see where nothing could be seen. The rain pattered against his armor.

Then another sound came, muffled by his helmet, through the hum of the wind in the cordage and the roar of the surf: the soughing of wind in trees. Marko peered. Directly below, he thought he could see the shifting ghostly-white band, which marked the surf against the base of the cliff. This ribbon slid under him and disappeared as the cliff edge occulted it. He should be over land. He pulled the valve cord.

It stuck.

He pulled with both hands. The rope gave all at once with a ripping sound and a loud hiss, and the bottom dropped out of the basket.

In the dark, Marko had pulled the rip cord by mistake, opening a slit several feet long in the upper part of the bag. The hot air rushed out and the balloon fell.

It struck with a crash, hurling Marko to the bottom of the basket. He had flexed his knees before striking, so no bones were broken. Still, the shock half stunned him, so that it took him several seconds to rise shakily to his feet.

He picked up his shield and climbed out of the basket, pushing through a tangle of ropes. He was on top of the cliff, all right, several feet back from the edge.

His next task was to light the little pyrotechnic flare the philosophers had given him, to signal them to sail around to the landing place. But rain had gotten into his tinder box. No matter how often he clicked the flint and steel lighter, it refused to light.

He gave up. The balloon could not be hauled back aboard the *Incredible*. If Halran tried to haul it back, it would merely be pulled off the cliff, to smash on the talus below and be lost in the sea. If Marko cut the rope, Halran would know from the slackening what had happened. At least he would know that the balloon was no longer attached. If Marko could tie a knot in the rope before letting it fall, those aboard would infer that he had landed safely and would bring the ship to the beach.

Marko took out his ax, got a grip on the rope, and chopped. At the third try he severed it.

The rope was slippery with the rain and much heavier than he expected. The weight of the long catenary snatched the end out of his grasp.

Marko sat down on the phosphor grass with his head in his hands. He almost wept with chagrin and vexation.

After a few minutes, he roused himself. His eyes had now adjusted to the darkness. Out to sea, he could just make out the black bulk of the *Incredible*. Would she put out to sea, for Niok or some other non-Eropian port, leaving him? He did not fear the witches in a stand-up fight, but he could not go without food and sleep indefinitely.

The guards would soon stumble upon the balloon and know that something was up. Well, he could fix that. He pushed the basket, foot by foot, until it toppled over the edge of the cliff, dragging the bag after it and almost taking Marko along by tangling him in its ropes. Halran would not like the loss of his contraption, but the balloon was of no present use and only increased his danger.

Marko looked out to sea again. The black shape was moving. At first he could not tell whither, but after a while it seemed to be headed to his left—towards the beach. An occasional red spark flew from its stack.

Marko walked towards the town of Mnaenn, paralleling the cliff edge but tramping across country. If he followed the cliff path, he would be too likely to meet an armed witch on her rounds. The ship traveled faster than he could walk in his ironmongery, but it had to detour to avoid rocks and shoals.

The rain beat against his helmet. His boots sank into the soft muddy soil and came out with sucking sounds. He detoured the town to reach the cliff on the south side, where the landing was.

At last he saw the section of cliff top he sought, with black silhouettes marking the location of the rope ladder. Voices came out of the murk:

". . . I saw them, I tell you. There's another!"

"You're mad, Als. What would sparks be flying around out there for?"

"You are near-sighted if you don't see them. We should report to the sergeant."

Marko stood still, hoping he was invisible in his black armor.

"Another thing," came a voice, "I could swear I've heard sounds as of armed men moving."

"Your imagination is inflamed, my dear. You should ..."

The muttered argument went on and on. Then one said:

"She's right, girls; there is a ship out there! Look!"

Marko stepped forward. The guards all had their backs to him. He thought there were three or four but could not be sure. He struck one over the head with the flat of his ax.

Clang! went the ax on the helmet. The guard dropped. Clang! went another. The other guards emitted piercing shrieks. Something clanked against Marko's shield, something else scraped his breastplate. There were footsteps running away and the jingle of accouterments. Other shouts answered from the village.

Marko felt around the rope ladder until he found the reel and the cord that held the crank. A chop severed the cord. Marko heaved on the crank, which turned, lowering the ladder down the face of the cliff. As the ladder unrolled, its increasing weight made the wheel revolve of its own accord.

Behind him, Marko heard the sound of armed witches approaching. He turned, letting the reel run on its own, and got out his ax again. With a great yammering, several of them came at him at once. He could barely see the points of their spears, which he caught on his shield.

The Great Fetish

"Get behind him!" shouted voices. "Surround him!" "Thrust for his crotch!" "He has lowered the ladder!"

One witch got too close. Marko stretched her senseless with the flat of his ax.

"Is he the only one?" "Crank up the ladder again!" "All together now, push him off the cliff!"

Marko shifted as fast as he could in the darkness so as not to present too easy a target. The darting points clicked and rasped against his defenses. From seaward came a hail.

"Hurry!" bellowed Marko. "You'll find the ladder down. I'm holding them off."

Clang, dzing, clank, went the witches' weapons against Marko's armor. Again and again he whirled, laying about him with his ax to beat them away from the ladder. One got a grip on his thigh. He struck her with his fist to knock her loose and heard her shriek as she fell off the cliff in the dark.

"They're coming up!" "Drop boulders on them!" "Cut the ropes of the ladder!" "The darkness is full of them!" "Get the rest of the women, or we are lost!"

Marko struggled on and on. Something sharp found the unarmored back of his left thigh, and the leg turned weak under him.

"All at him at once!" "Fetch the Stringiarch!" "Get some lanterns!" "*Eee*, there's another behind us!"

Marko leaned against the reel of the ladder to take the weight off his injured leg.

"One more try!" panted a witch officer. "Push him off the cliff!"

Marko limped around the reel, stumbling over the

witches he had knocked down and swinging his ax. He roared: "Curse you, stand back or I'll give you the edge! I've been sparing you, but I won't much longer!"

Lanterns bobbed in the darkness. A voice called: "Stand back to let us shoot!"

Marko dropped to one knee beside the reel, holding his iron shield up in front of him. Presently there was a snap of bowstrings, and a thrum of quarrels. Several sharp hammer blows struck the shield. Another grazed his helmet.

"Get around to the side. He cannot face all ways at once."

Something moved behind Marko. He rose, turning and raising his ax.

"Is that you, Master Prokopiu?" said the deep voice of Ulf Toskano. Others crowded up behind him. The philosophers opened out into an armored rank and surged forwards. For an instant there arose the clangor of weapons on armor, and then with cries of despair the witches broke and fled.

※※※

"Aye," said the Stringiarch, sitting on a chair in the Temple of Einstein before the philosophers. "I know the true story of the Descent, at least as it has been handed down from stringiarch to stringiarch." She glared up at the semicircle of intent faces, shiny with sweat and wet in the lamplight. "If I tell you brigands, will you spare my girls?"

"We had no intention—" began Toskano, but Marko poked him and interrupted:

"If you tell the truth, madam, no harm shall befall your charges. But take care, for we have means of confirming or refuting your story."

"Very well. The story, as it has come down to me, is as follows: Before the Descent, the men of Earth had become so many that there was not enough land to support them. So their gods ordered them to build two great ships, promising that when the ships were finished they, the gods, would waft them through the empty space between that world and this—"

"She means the ships of space I told you about," interrupted Bivar. "And the gods were nothing but the leaders political."

Katlin glared at the little Iverianan but continued: "In time the ships set out from Earth. Between them they carried nearly two hundred people, as well as the female young of several domestic animals of that world and spells for causing them to conceive and bear without the presence of the male. Also seeds, tools, and other needful things. The gods' commands were to land both ships on Kforri and set up a settlement for colonization and study. Then the crews of both ships should enter one of the two, and the gods would take it back to Earth.

"Whether the gods became tired of carrying these great heavy ships so many millions of miles, and dropped them in trying to set them down, I do not know. But in any case both vessels were damaged on landing, to a degree that prevented their returning. However, there was little harm to the people in the ships, who therefore disembarked and set up the colony as planned. They hoped that, when the single ship failed to return at the appointed time, Earth would build another ship and persuade the gods to carry it to Kforri to find out what became of them.

"Here trouble arose. While the crews of the ships were all men, the settlers, who were all philosophers and men picked for their skill in colonization, had wives. The settlers said that, as the gods had so arranged matters, there was nothing to be done about it.

"But the crewmen lusted after the wives of the settlers. A machinist, Hasan Barmada, said that the gods had all gone back to Earth and deserted the colonists, and that therefore no attention need be paid to their commands. He formed a conspiracy and by a sudden uprising his men slew nearly all the male colonists, as well as their own officers who sided with the colonists. When the fighting was over there were about a hundred persons left on Kforri, a few more men than women.

"The crewmen took the wives of the colonists for their own and begat their kind. Because they had blasphemed and sinned against the gods, the gods did not inspire them with wisdom. They neglected the knowledge that the philosophers had brought with them from Earth, and in two generations had sunk to the level of barbarians.

"Also, they quarreled among themselves and split up into seven different tribes, according to the parts of Earth they had originally come from. Thus men from those parts that spoke Old Anglonian—places called Britain, Ireland, North America, and some others—formed the Anglonian tribe. Men from the land of Europe formed Eropia. Men from the islands of Russia and Balka formed

Vizantia, named for the Balkan city of Byzantium. And so our modern nations arose.

"One philosopher who had much divine blood in his veins, an Anglonian named David Grant, escaped from the massacre with some of the women and the cards composing the Great Fetish. On Earth, there was a magical instrument for reading these cards. Whether such an instrument had been brought to Kforri and then broken I do not know, but in any case David Grant had no such device with him. Nevertheless, he hoped that something would happen to make these records of Earthly wisdom available once again—"

"It was called micrography," said Bivar.

"He came to this island on a raft," continued the Stringiarch, "with several women who fled from their new mates. His descendants built this temple. He told his wives and children about the gods of Earth and about their duty to preserve this divine wisdom. The earthly god whom he most admired, Einstein, became after his death the special patron god of Mnaenn.

"David Grant, or Devgran as he is now called in common speech, begat many daughters but no sons. Hence, an all-woman settlement came into being. Since the women feared and hated the men of the mainland because they had slain their own true husbands, they resolved never to let any settle on Mnaenn. From that day to this the settlement has kept up its numbers in the manner you know."

Domingo Bivar asked: "Pardon, madam, one question. If we are descended from a few crewmen, how do we have so many surnames different?"

"During the early generations, the people did not follow the Earthly custom of giving all children of one marriage the same surname, because there were so few of them that such names would not have been distinctive. Instead, they gave them names of other men whom they had known or heard about on Earth. Thus many were named for famous Earthly men, gods, and demigods. Others received made-up names, or were named for their attributes or occupations. After a while they reverted to the original custom. Even so there are, for example, many thousands of Bivars in Iveriana besides yourself, Doctor."

"Thank you," said Bivar. "There are some places anomalous in your narrative, but I am sure that when we transcribe the records, rational explanations of everything will transpire."

Katlin spoke bitterly to Marko: "Master Prokopiu, I did not believe you when you claimed, just now, you were the prophesied son of Mnaenn, come back to read the Fetish and end the stringiarchate. I am sure no man-child could have been born and smuggled off the island, as you assert; our control is too close in such matters. However, you can read the cards with the instrument of these Mingkworen. And whereas we are in your power, I suppose we might as well put the best face on things. What will you do with us? Throw us over the cliff, as you did poor Lizveth?"

Marko did not himself really believe the son-of-Mnaenn story but had thought it up to give the witches a graceful excuse for surrendering. He looked at Toskano, who said:

"Not at all, madam. We regret the death of that witch. We did not mean to hurt any of you."

"Soft words will never right the wrong of your deeds."

Toskano said: "True, madam, some consciences among us are not altogether at ease. But then, by your practice of male infanticide, which would fill most people with horror, and by your unjust treatment of Messrs. Halran and Prokopiu when they unwittingly trespassed on your land, you have given up your claim to sympathy."

"What do you intend?"

"Oh, some of us will return to our own countries. Others, especially those from Eropia, will stay here and set up a philosophical republic. Among them are enough single ones to provide husbands for such of your girls as wish them."

"Hm," said ex-Stringiarch Katlin, wrinkling her nose in disgust. "If our traditions speak true, the men of Earth tried to set up such an ideal government many times but never succeeded for long. That, however, is your problem."

※※※

Marko had no chance for more than a brief greeting with Sinthi that night. He had much to do, his wound hurt, and he was tired out. He learned that, when the rope had been hauled back aboard the *Incredible*, its cut end told of Marko's safe landing and led Toskano to bring the ship to the beach.

Next morning, leaning on a stick, Marko stood on the edge of the cliff watching Muphrid rise. A little way off, Boert Halran was looking over the edge and lamenting the destruction of his beautiful balloon. Domingo Bivar was kneading Marko's arm and talking excitedly of the wonderful things the philosophers would do when all the records of the Fetish had been transcribed.

"We shall build a ship of space of our own and fly back to Earth to see why they have forgotten us!" he cried. "It is wonderful! The rest of the Fetish includes books innumerable—on history, science, language, everything. There are even sections of fiction and verse . . ."

Marko, who disliked the little man's effusiveness, disengaged his arm as Sinthi came by. He thought her the most attractive object he had seen in years.

"Hello," he said. "You see, I came back as I promised."

"That is right. Where are you going now?"

"Well, since the stringiarchate is over, I thought I might stay here. While I didn't really do anything, the philosophers seem to think me worthy of their company."

"I heard they chose you Prez or something."

"No, not quite. They want me to be a kind of vice-manager under Toskano. I was even thinking of sending for my mother."

"Oh. You were going to take me away, weren't you? You promised."

"Well . . . I suppose. . . . Look, maybe we can figure out something just as good. You see, ah . . ."

They stood, Marko looking down and Sinthi up. Marko had a feeling that she would not mind if he grabbed her right there. Instead, he stared into space, shifted his feet, blushed, gulped, stammered, and finally said:

"Let's walk along the cliff path. I'm sure I have many interesting things to tell you about."

They strolled off without bothering to excuse themselves to Domingo Bivar. Marko was limping and talking volubly. Presently he was holding Sinthi's hand. Bivar, looking after them, sighed a romantic sigh, brushed his hair out of his eyes, and hurried off to find another arm to knead.

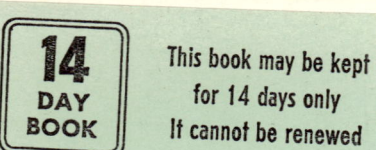

This book may be kept for 14 days only. It cannot be renewed

NOV 1978

SF

c-1

De Camp, Lyon Sprague, 1907–
   The great fetish / L. Sprague De Camp.
New York : Doubleday, 1978.
   177 p. ; 22 cm.

CAMBRIA COUNTY LIBRARY
Johnstown, Pa. 15901

FINES PER DAY:
Adults 5¢, Children 2¢

I. Title

PJo   JOCBxc   78-1239